HEIKKI HEIKKINEN

Heikki Heikkinen

and Other Stories of Upper Peninsula Finns

by

Lauri Anderson

NORTH STAR PRESS OF ST. CLOUD, INC.

1-320-253-1636

Cover Photo: Courtesy of Len and Norma Ojala.

ISBN: 0-87839-097-9

Printed in the United States of America by Versa Press, Inc. of East Peoria,
Illinois.

Published by: North Star Press of St. Cloud, Inc.
                P.O. Box 451
                St. Cloud, Minnesota 56302

Dedication

For Beverly, Charlotte, Lucy
Eric and Timo.

Contents

An Odd Collection of Finns

Becoming a Finn

The Author ·

Very early in life, I became aware of my Finnishness. Our little Upper Peninsula town was full of Finns. Blues and whites were everywhere. Our home was white with blue trim. The Lutheran church was white with blue trim. The high school athletic uniforms were white with blue trim. As a small child, I was often dressed in blue and white. Formal meals were served on a blue-and-white tablecloth. Ma's best china was blue and white. So was her kitchen. Later, when I discovered baseball, I cheered for the Dodgers because I figured they must be Finns in those nifty blue-and-white uniforms.

In my boyhood, I had only two national flags on my wall—Finland's and the Upper Peninsula's. Everyone knew the Upper Peninsula was five times bigger than the Lower.

I also knew I was a Finn because all fish in our house were pickled, all potatoes were boiled, and the Jell-O had to have plenty of dill.

When my parents drove to town to get necessities, Pa took his ax. Non-Finns didn't do that, but my Finnish dad always said, "You never know when an ax might come in handy." We honked at every passing SISU bumper sticker.

When my neighbors and relatives took a vacation by plane, they always flew west to go east. They'd pick up a chartered FinnAir flight out of Duluth. The charter flew nonstop to Helsinki and straight back to Duluth, avoiding all dens of iniquity, such as Paris or New York. If Finnish neighbors went on vacation by car, they drove to Lake Worth, Florida—never to Fort Lauderdale or Miami. Naturally, Lake Worth was full of Finns. When they came back, they'd often dropped five hundred bucks on a funny-looking blue-and-white Finnish national costume.

Our town was full of one-hundred percent Americans with names

1

like Wiitila, Ponkala, Viik, Koski, and Maki. Especially Maki. Makis were all over the place—in the woods cutting popple, in the bars drinking Stroh's, in the churches singing hymns, and in the saunas beating each other with sticks. Everywhere I turned, there were Makis or reminders of Makis. I don't want to make a mountain out of a molemaki, but what in the Sam Maki were Makis doing in so many places? On the radio, I'd hear Makibilly music about those "Oklahoma Makis where I was born." We'd play baseball with a Makirich-and-Bradsby bat, and I learned to ski on the bunnymaki. On the way to town, one sign read, "Steep Maki Use Low Gear," and another read "Don't Pass on a Maki." For breakfast Ma and Pa had Maki Brothers coffee, which Pa said was cheap but wasn't worth a Maki of beans. At school, we learned about the Black Makis of South Dakota. Makis abounded in our reading, from Jack and Jill, who ran up the Maki, to Ernest Hemingway's *Green Makis of Africa*.

When I first went to school, I thought Jones and Smith were very weird names, but Hautamaki was okay.

In school, when the teacher talked about a superior education, I knew she meant learning how to fish on a big lake. When the teacher talked about a major institution of higher learning, the Jones kid thought she meant Harvard, and the Smith kid thought she meant the state university in Ann Arbor, but I knew better. She meant Suomi College.

I learned Finnish sports early, so when the other kids in school talked about skiing, I knew what they meant—to run as fast as you could across a flat field with long sticks tied to your boots.

Eventually, I was old enough to take my Finnish Pa's advice and believe everything a non-Finn told me and disbelieve everything a Finn told me.

I drank gallons of coffee every day, ate cold cooked beets for school lunch and thought of Vaino instead of Herbert when the teacher talked of Hoover. I ate Vicks Vapo-Rub in the winter as a preventive measure.

Now that I'm on the downMaki side of forty, I avoid Maki-isms wherever they appear. I refuse to watch TV shows like "Maki Street Blues." Instead I watch old movies like *The Long Hot Sauna, Helmi and Her Sisters, Return of the Pink Poikka, Urho's Big Adventure, Raaki* (dat poxing movie), and *Dirty Ari*. My favorite song is "Who's Saari Now?"

I completed my education by taking pre-Finnish studies at Suomi College. Pre-Finnish studies is for those non-Finns and half-Finns (that's me!) striving diligently to be one-hundred percent Finn but lack necessary qualifications. Maybe they aren't Lutheran or they've never cut down a tree. Or they don't like coffee! Maybe it's because they can hold their booze. Or maybe they smile a lot, touch and are friendly.

After intensive study, I passed the final exam with flying colors (blue and white, naturally). For the question that asked me to list churches, I put Apostolic, ELCA, Missouri Synod, Wisconsin Synod, and ALC. None of those Methodists or Presbyterians for me! For the question about what to do on Saturday night, I put sauna! For the question about a famous general, I put Mannerheim. And so on.

Now I'm a professor of humanities at Suomi College. I am a representative of Finnish-American culture. I write important papers on important subjects, with titles like, "Orpheus Really Played the Kantele," "Saunas in San Francisco and AIDS—A Correlation?" "Vainamoinen Misspelled—Suomi College Variations and the New Semiotics," "Vodka and Herring—Two Sources of Pickling for Finns," and, finally, "Visions of Vodka: Mass Hysteria in an Apostolic Community."

I've come a long way in my Finnishness. My daddy would be proud!

Sam Dorvinen

Sam Dorvinen was a fourth-generation Finn. Sam knew practically from birth that his precursors had been rugged individualists because his dad told him about earlier generations every Saturday night during sauna. His dad usually saunaed with a fifth of Finnish vodka on the bench beside him and with an invisible cloud of steam nipping at his hair and skin. The old man was usually as red as a side of beef and as pickled as herring by the time he exited. In between, he told exciting stories about the old days, about life on isolated farms or in wilderness cabins. In the old man's stories, every self-respecting Finn had driven a pick-up and had worked in the woods or in the mines. Every tough old guy had eaten pickled eggs, pickled fish, and beef jerky at the Mosquito Inn. Every one of them had guzzled gallons of Stroh's mixed with cheap brandy. They had all worn ragged and stained flannel shirts all year round as a sign of their fortitude, their *sisu*. On Sunday, every one of them had watched "Finland Calling" on Channel Six early in the morning and then had gone to the Lutheran church to clear his account with the Lord before beginning another round of hard work and booze on Monday morning.

Sam's Finnishness was greatly diluted. He couldn't even speak the language, and, as a child, he couldn't imagine living anywhere other than in his room in his parents' house in South Range, Michigan. Sam rode a ten-speed bike when he needed to get somewhere, which usually wasn't far since all of South Range was within a five-minute ride of his parents' home on Second Street. As a boy, Sam couldn't imagine working in the woods or in the mines because he hated black flies and closed-in spaces. He preferred pizza, Twinkies, and Coke to pickled eggs and beer. He wore T-shirts emblazoned with Snoopy or Big Bird all year round, and, on Sundays, he slept until noon and then watched a ball game on TV.

As a boy, Sam tried to become more of a Finn by reading and rereading the *Kalevala* in the Kirby translation of 1907. He sometimes quoted it at inopportune times. When he fell madly in love in eighth grade with one of the many Vainio girls, he passed her a note in math class. The note said, "Let the tender blade spring upward, / Let the earth support and cherish . . . / That the corn might sprout up stronger, / And the stalks might wave and rustle."

The Vainio girl passed the note hurriedly to the teacher and fled the room in tears. Poor Sam had to confront the teacher, the principal, the superintendent and, later, a delegation of irate parents and his dad's belt. Sam tried to explain that the lines described Vainamoinen sowing his seed, but that just made things worse. "The next time your blade springs up, keep it to yourself," his father yelled.

As a teenager, Sam had a bad attitude toward other ethnic groups. He probably got his attitude from his dad, who hadn't spoken to his Hungarian neighbor in forty years. Sam's dad saw no reason why he should speak to someone who had been dead wrong all of his life and whose ancestors had been dead wrong for a thousand years before that. "A long time ago in Central Asia," his dad had explained to Sam, "we Finns and the Hungarians had a common God-given tongue and culture. Then one day the Hungarians rejected Finnish, Finnishness, and life in the north woods and moved to the Danube to play violins. Heck, they aren't even Lutheran," his dad had explained. "When our neighbor admits that he's really a Finn who made a mistake, I'll speak to him," the old man had said.

By his teens, Sam wore his Finnishness like a badge of honor. Through his T-shirts, he was always daring the world to insult his heritage. One shirt proclaimed that Sam had SISU. Another proclaimed that he had FINN POWER. A third had THANK GOD on the front and I'M A FINN on the back. In addition, Sam always carried a long Finnish hunter's knife, a *puukko*, on his belt. The only liquor he would drink was an occasional nip of Finlandia vodka. On Saturday nights at the Uphill, a hard-rock hangout for college students, he only danced the Negaunee schottische.

At Jeffers High School, Sam admired the Finnish boys from Misery Bay, all of whom wore black leather jackets and drove old junk cars with noisy or missing mufflers. On the backs of their leather jackets the Misery Bay guys had devil's heads, dice, or skulls and crossed bones.

Sam asked for and received a black leather jacket for Christmas when he was a junior. He also got a black leather motorcycle hat as an extra. The hat had a winged wheel in the middle of the brim. With his allowance, Sam added a pair of tall black engineer's boots to his paraphernalia. When Sam's Uncle Toivo saw him in his new outfit, he snickered. "What the hell did you do, join the foreign legion?" Uncle Toivo asked. Then he added, "When they let you out, I want those boots."

Sam searched for an appropriate Finnish symbol to emblazon on the back of his jacket. At Kukkonen's Finnish wares shop, in among the Arabian salad bowls and the sauna soaps, he found a decal of Santa, his sleigh, and eight tiny reindeer. Sam bought the decal, cut off Santa and his sleigh, and implanted the eight tiny reindeer on the back of his jacket. At Jeffers, Sam tried to explain to the Finnish guys from Misery Bay that the reindeer were symbolic of Lapland and the Arctic tundra, but they wouldn't buy that interpretation. "Which one is Prancer?" one of them asked, and the rest guffawed.

By the time Sam was a senior, he was desperate to assert himself as a rugged individualist Finn. A number of the Misery Bay Finnish guys in his class were already working in the woods with their dads. They made the ten-mile trip to school on their new Harley-Davidson motorcycles in the fall or in their old junk cars in the winter. They smelled strongly of pitch and sawdust, and their flannel shirts were stained and ragged. They already smoked Marlboros, drank Stroh's on Saturday night, and dated blonde-haired, fair-skinned girls with joyous laughs.

Sam had his baseball card collection, his ten-speed bike, and his need to leave his mark on the world.

The summer after graduation, Sam asked a couple of loggers if they needed an extra worker, but they just looked at Sam and laughed. He eventually found employment in the K-Mart deli at the Copper Country Mall. He made sub sandwiches and oatmeal cookies in the deli and occasionally sold hot dogs at the store entrance when there were sales. Sometimes the Misery Bay guys came into K-Mart with their girl friends. Occasionally one said hello, but mostly they ignored Sam. None ever bought his oatmeal cookies.

Sam longed to impress the Misery Bay guys. He decided to shop around for a new car because he knew none of them could afford one. Unfortunately, Sam couldn't afford one either. Then one day when Sam and his mother were shopping in Marquette, Sam spotted a Yugo dealership. At last he had found a new car that he could afford. Plus the company had just gone belly up because its main plant was under siege from snipers and heavy artillery in Sarajevo. Sam got a brand-new car for under two thousand dollars. He was the proud owner of a tiny, pea-green Yugo sedan.

For the next couple of weeks, Sam improved his Yugo by spray painting orange flames onto the rear fenders, painting FINN POWER onto the rear bumper, and hanging a pair of dice the size of small pillows on his rearview mirror. On the hood he wrote MADE IN AMERICA WITH FINNISH PARTS in bold alternating blue and white letters. Sam felt proud when he heard a neighbor, Wilho Maki, refer to Sam's car as the Yugo from hell. Sam didn't realize that Wilho was speaking in jest. "You're the Upper Peninsula's answer to Hell's Angels," Wilho told Sam, and Sam stuck out his chest proudly.

On the Fourth of July, Sam drove his Yugo to Toivola and turned right onto the Misery Bay road. He drove to Agate Beach, parked, and spent several hours lying on the beach under layers of sunscreen. Occasionally, he plunged into the frigid waters of Lake Superior. Then the Misery Bay guys appeared on their motorcycles at the far end of the beach. They came roaring toward Sam, their huge Harleys spraying sand and driftwood. Their leader was Chris Koski, a short but very broad kid with a big chest and big shoulders. Chris brought his bike to a sliding halt a yard or so from Sam, spraying him with grit. "Is that your car?" Chris asked Sam, pointing at the Yugo.

Sam admitted that it was.

"Every Finn in America is embarrassed by you and that car," said Chris. "Just the other night a cousin of mine called from Fairport Harbor, Ohio, just to tell me that he'd heard about your damned car. I've gotten postcards from other cousins in Cloquet, Minnesota; Butte, Montana; Lake Worth, Florida; and Fitchburg, Massachusetts. Every one of 'em wanted to tell me how embarrassed they were as Finns because of your car."

Sam didn't know what to say. His face began to burn with shame. Chris reached into his Harley saddlebag and withdrew a spray can of black paint. "We don't want to hurt your feelings, Sam, but no self-respecting young Finnish guy would drive a Yugo, especially one with flames on the fenders. An Uncle Toivo might, just because he was too cheap to buy something more expensive—but not some young guy with any sense of self-worth. Hell, I'd rather you drove a used logging truck or a Zamboni than a Yugo."

Another of the Misery Bay bikers spoke up. "I've got cousins in South Paris, Maine, and Walla Walla, Washington," he said.

"Don't tell me," interrupted Sam. "They wrote to tell you that they'd heard about my car."

"That's right," said the biker.

Chris climbed off his bike and walked over to the Yugo with the spray can of black paint. He sprayed over the FINN POWER on the back bumper. Then he sprayed over the MADE IN AMERICA WITH FINNISH PARTS on the hood. "Get rid of the car," he said to Sam as he returned to his Harley, climbed aboard, and slipped it into gear. Then he and his friends roared off down the beach.

Sam returned to South Range a bitter young man. He gave the Yugo to Mrs. Koskiniemi, a retired neighbor lady who gardened. She had her grandson remove the Yugo's roof with a torch. Then he drove the Yugo into the corner of her lawn and filled it with dirt so Mrs. Koskiniemi could use it as a planter for dozens of red and white geraniums. In August, she won a blue ribbon from the Range Gardening Club for having the most unusual display.

Sam gave his black leather jacket to Josh Heinonen, a ten-year-old neighbor with some artistic ability. Josh added pink, yellow and red Power Rangers to the eight tiny reindeer.

Sam quit his job at K-Mart, left South Range, and became a student of Finnish language and culture at Suomi College in Hancock. The admissions counselor assumed that Sam was a Finn because of his major and because of his name, but Sam insisted that he wasn't. "Sure, I have some Finnish blood," Sam explained, "but it's so diluted by America that I'm not really a Finn. I lack *sisu*, and I lack a soul. I need to learn how to be a Finn by taking these courses." Sam insisted that, until he graduated, he did not wish to be called a Finn. "I want to be incognito in the dorm," he said. "I'm going to tell the other Finnish students that I'm half Latvian and half Cherokee. I'm going to use the Native American name of Screaming Eagle."

"That's pretty loony," said the admissions counselor, "but no loonier than a lot of other stuff our students pull."

Eventually, Sam graduated and moved on to the University of Minnesota, where he received his B.A. and M.A. He earned his Ph.D. at Indiana University and became a professional Finn.

Now he's in the vanguard of Finnish culture in America. He writes important papers on anything and everything Finnish. Recently, he wrote a sociological study of Misery Bay Finns. He called it, "Delusions of Grandeur—Flannel Shirts and Harleys in a Psychopathic Community."

No one in Misery Bay read the article. No one there was even aware that it existed. Generally people in Misery Bay are not among the three hundred fifty subscribers to the *American Journal of Psychopathic Studies.*

Sam is once again proud of his Finnishness. He drives a 1950 Ford Mustang painted blue and white like the Finnish flag. The car is worth many times its original price as new. The Misery Bay crowd would be in awe of the car. They would approve.

Eddie Maki

Eddie Maki's hometown, Coppertown, sat at the head of a long, narrow bay of Lake Superior on the Keweenaw Peninsula in northern Michigan. Coppertown's few businesses extended on pilings over the water. The businesses were old and had fake square fronts like a Hollywood movie set of the Old West. The businesses were not in good shape. Paint peeled, roofs sank in the middle, corners sagged. There were two gas stations, a fire station, a general store, a barber shop, a coffee shop, a light-and-power company, three grocery stores, and two churches—the Lutheran and the Pentecostal.

On a rise at the north end of town sat the high school, a venerable old building with a history dating back to the late eighteen hundreds. But the wooden school, like the town, was dying.

Eddie's father ran the smallest of the three grocery stores. Most of his profits came from beer and meat. On Sundays, he sold a dozen or more cases of vanilla extract (68.5 percent alcohol) because an ordinance made the town dry on the Sabbath. After church in summer, the miners gathered along the lakeshore behind Eddie's father's store and passed around the small extract bottles. They tossed down the highly perfumed stuff as if they were tossing down shots of vodka. They tossed the empty bottles into the bay. The water was shallow and the bottom sandy. Thousands of tiny bottles lay scattered over the lake bottom. On sunny days they glinted like stars.

Winters in Eddie Maki's hometown were long and bitter, with January temperatures well below zero. Snow accumulations routinely reached three hundred inches. Spring arrived late, at the beginning of what should have been summer. Summers were brief but beautiful—long cool days that faded slowly into evenings full of loon calls and brush strokes of wind through the trees. Fall commenced with a few days of glorious color, but the leaves soon fell and the remainder consisted of dead brown days under cold, leaden skies.

Eddie's father was a second-generation Finn, his mother a proud, transplanted New Englander. Eddie's mother's family had invested heavily in the local copper mines. Her people owned a cottage on shore property along Lake Superior. She had met Joe Maki at a dance when her family was vacationing.

Eddie's Finnish grandparents spoke little English. They lived in the log farmhouse Eddie's grandfather had built when he came from Finland. They attended the Lutheran church when the service was in Finnish. They had odd customs and ate strange food—pickled fish, yogurt, heavy dark bread with smelt inside.

Eddie's mother's people lived through history. They traced their roots back to the original colonies. They drank only milk or water and ate plain food without seasoning—roast beef, boiled vegetables, potatoes, and beans. They attended a Congregational Church, joined philanthropic community clubs, and did not associate with newly-arrived immigrants such as Eddie's Finnish grandparents. They lived downstate in Detroit, longed for Boston, and had never seen the log home that Eddie's father had built with logs cut from his own land.

In the 1950s, the Maki home was the only one in Coppertown with indoor plumbing, bath, and shower. Eddie's mother came from money and hated outmoded and outdated ways. She always had the best—the latest model refrigerator, a dishwasher, a washer and dryer, a freezer.

The Finnish women still washed in tubs. They still hung out their wash, even in winter, when they'd bring in the sheets and clothes stiff as glass and hang them in their kitchens to complete the drying. The Finnish women still used root cellars and did their personal business in an outhouse.

In addition to being a sound businessman and a superb carpenter, Eddie's father hunted deer and bear and made gloves, leggings, and hats from the tanned hides. He raised cattle, lambs, and chickens. He slaughtered them and prepared them for the freezer. He caught trout summer and winter. He raised a vegetable garden, and Eddie's mother canned and pickled. The Maki store was popular with Finns because Eddie's father stocked Finnish foods, made his own blood sausage, pickled his own tripe, and salted his own salmon. He spoke their language and understood their wants.

Eddie's mother hated the Finns for their earthiness. She saw them as still trapped by the peasant mindsets they had brought from Scandinavia. She admitted that they had some admirable traits—industriousness, parsimoniousness, and honesty—but she abhorred their weekend drunkenness, their lack of social graces, and their ignorance of the world outside the town.

Eddie's mother found Finnish incomprehensible and Finnish food disgusting. She prepared the same plain foods that her mother had prepared. She refused to make any un-American foods except spaghetti and pizza, but her Italian cooking had a peculiar New England flavor from the bits of salt pork added to the sauce. Eddie's father abhorred his wife's cooking. Often he prepared Finnish food, which he and Eddie ate together. Eddie's mother could not comprehend how anyone could eat fish roe in eggs, animal organs, or fish preserved in lye. Yet she had married a man who ate all these things. Still, she recognized that she had gotten a good husband. Eddie's father didn't drink, didn't dance the polka on Saturday night at the Finn Hall, didn't gamble, and went with her to the Lutheran Church. Mostly he worked. He opened his store every day, seven days a week at eight a.m. Usually he didn't close it until eleven p.m.

When Eddie's father was home, Eddie's mother ranted at him, her mouth never closed, and her voice never soft. She accused him of having no ambition, of never earning enough to satisfy her need to be socially above all her neighbors. She blamed him for every little thing that went wrong. If the cellar flooded during the spring run-off, it was because he had chosen to live in such a godforsaken place. If he took an afternoon off in the summer to drive his family to a picnic area, he drove too fast or too slow or wasn't ready on time. In her eyes, her husband could never do anything right.

Eddie's mother mentioned again and again that she and Eddie were from a proud old New England family with a history dating back to before the Revolution. she told Eddie again and again that she and he didn't fit in with the Finns, that their worlds were small compared to theirs.

She read a lot—three or four thick books a month, mostly historical novels. She knew a lot of history and instilled in Eddie her love for literature and for the past. At bedtime, she read Eddie books about the Revolutionary period. By the time Eddie was ready for school, he could tell the other kids stories about Benedict Arnold's march through Maine to attack Quebec. He could explain vividly how Arnold got lost on the Dead River. Usually the other kids weren't interested. Neither were their parents.

Often Eddie lay awake late into the night as he listened to his mother verbally attack his father. Her voice roared like a storm through their small home. Eddie pictured his father nodding agreement or ducking aside, trying to make the barrage of words stop. But it was to no avail. She hated the town and blamed him for her unhappiness. Yet Eddie sensed that she too was to blame. She was paralyzed by her own sense of who she should be. She could not accept that she was a housewife married to a small-town store owner in a cold and uncompromising corner of the world.

As Eddie lay abed, he would pray for his mother to shut up. When he was little, sometimes he would cry. He didn't want his mother to do or say things that made him hate her because, of course, he loved her very deeply. She was usually a good mother. She fed him well, clothed him well, and doctored him when he was sick. She surrounded him with books and instilled in him the need to know a larger world. She fed Eddie her own need to know about things. And, though she didn't realize it, she also gave him a distrust of women. He assumed all of them were as explosive as his mother.

❖   ❖   ❖   ❖   ❖

All the years that Eddie was growing up, the Finns of Coppertown talked about *sisu*. Eddie asked his Finnish relatives to define *sisu*. Eddie's Uncle Wilho defined *sisu* as guts. As a small child, Eddie often heard Wilho's *sisu* rumbling after his uncle had consumed too much vodka and pickled fish. Eddie's Uncle Toivo defined *sisu* as stubbornness, but that only confused little Eddie. He knew that mules were famous for their stubbornness, but did that mean that they had *sisu*? Eddie's dad defined *sisu* as determination—as choosing a goal and then working toward it in an intelligent way.

Eddie's dad, like the other Finns in the town, really meant choosing a *practical* goal. They wanted their children to value reading and writing because then they could become lawyers or businessmen or insurance agents or Husqvarna dealers. They desperately wanted their kids to escape from a life in the mines, but they weren't particularly interested in any kid who learned to read and write so that later he could go to college to study philosophy, literature, or art. It was okay to pick up a little music knowledge on the side, if you had the talent, but the knowledge should stop with the polka and with some Finnish hymns. The polka could earn a guy a hundred bucks on Saturday night at the Range Lounge, and the hymns could earn a guy another fifty at the funeral of some old-country type.

Eddie wasn't much interested in practicality. Right from the beginning, he was a lot more interested in the meanings of things. Every Sunday morning, Eddie's mother forced him into a suit and tie and trundled him off to the Lutheran church. Eddie hated the services. He found them boring. The music was too slow, the sermons too serious, and the people too stiff. His mother, however, insisted that attendance was practical. "Say your prayers and go to church and one day you can go to Lutheran Heaven," she said.

"Yes, but what does it mean—to be in a Lutheran Heaven?" Eddie wanted to know. He'd been reading the *National Geographic* at the time and knew he'd rather be in Tahiti.

One Sunday, when his mother stopped at the drug store to pick up some cod liver oil and some Vicks Vapo-rub in preparation for the yearly onslaught of winter colds, Eddie stopped at the wire rack by the door and read the tabloid headlines. He was especially taken by one headline—MINISTER EXPLODES DURING SERMON. The subheading said, CONGREGATION SURPRISED BY FORCE OF BLAST. Eddie wished that something like that would happen during their Sunday service. "It would really perk up our stiff-necked old Finns," he thought.

As a boy, Eddie often needed a bit of perking up himself. He was often dissatisfied with the limited entertainment of a small town. At the same time, he was aware that in some ways his hometown was unique. For example, a set of moose horns were nailed to a post a couple of miles south of town. The town's founder had shot the moose back in the eighteen hundreds and had nailed the horns to a tree as a trail marker. Now the preserved horns were a minor tourist attraction.

A tiny museum on the third floor of the fire station was also unique. The museum honored locally famous poachers such as Arvo Heikkinen. The museum contained a photo of Arvo standing in front of a huge tree decorated as if for Christmas with the carcasses of thirty-two deer and a bear. Another honored poacher had shot two wardens from out of town in 1910 when the wardens threatened to shoot the poacher's best deer hound.

The copper mines honeycombing the town were the third special feature. The mines reminded Eddie of the pervasiveness of death. Eddie's youth in the 1950s was haunted by death—by miners crushed by falling slabs of rock, by miners plummeting to their doom because a cable had snapped. With each death, the surviving miners and their families absorbed their grief without fanfare and quietly attended the Lutheran church. A few of the seedier families—those with too many children and too many junked cars in the yard—saw visions, were born again, and attended the Pentecostal church, where they wailed out their pain in emotion-laden hymns and damnation sermons. Many miners gave up on life altogether and drank themselves into oblivion every weekend.

When Eddie was eight, the next-door neighbor had a lung removed. Except for a circle the size of a grapefruit, the removed lung was completely impacted with mine dust. The miner kept the lung in a jar on the kitchen table. Little Eddie, among others, hefted it and marveled at its weight. A few months later the other lung hemorrhaged, and the neighbor drowned in seconds.

Most miners expected this death by silicosis. They were not surprised to be incapacitated at forty-five or fifty. The incapacitated ex-miners sat listlessly in the entranceways of stores and gasped for breath. Others sought a self-inflicted end, usually through uncontrolled non-stop drunkenness but sometimes through more immediate means. When Eddie was nine, an unemployed illiterate miner who lived with his wife and five children at the corner of Eddie's street blew his brains out with a hunting rifle. When Eddie was ten, the woman across the street tacked to the front door a note for her high school-age daughter. "Go get your father" is all it said. The girl came home from school, checked the door, found it locked, and entered the house through a window. She found her mother a suicide by pistol shot, slumped naked in the bathtub. Eddie and the other neighborhood children were waiting when the girl came outside. Eddie remembered that the girl had been more shocked by her mother's nakedness than by her death. The girl had said over and over, "Why didn't she have the decency to wear her robe or something?"

✿   ✿   ✿   ✿   ✿

By the time he entered high school, Eddie already knew that he did not want to remain in Coppertown. He saw high school as something that he had to get through before he went far away from mines and miners. In many ways, he admired the miners. After all, they knew how to use and repair heavy machinery, how to handle explosives, how to follow a vein of copper deep into the earth. They also were handy with wood and with vehicles and were eminently practical in a thousand other ways.

But their practicality didn't seem to get them anywhere. Eddie saw his own hope in being impractical. After all, his mother's people were all impractical, and they had lots of money. Eddie spent a lot of time in the town's tiny library, beneath the stairwell in the fire station. Mrs. Jarvi, the librarian, frequently ordered books especially for Eddie from the state library in Lansing. Eddie read Jack Kerouac, John Steinbeck, Ernest Hemingway, and Dostoevsky. He read European history and dabbled with French, but that wasn't nearly impractical enough. Eddie sent for the official State Department program for learning Hausa, a West African language. He studied the text and listened to tapes and drove his father crazy by greeting him in Hausa. "Sanu," he'd say. "Ina aiki?"

Eddie's father would reply with a Finnish curse. "Why don't you learn a useful language, like Finnish?" he said. "Why do you ignore your own heritage?"

Eddie reacted by refusing to eat his father's favorite foods— *mojakka, nisu,* and *sillikaviaari.* Briefly he tried vegetarianism and Tibetan Buddhism. He began to collect Bulgarian coins, Orange Free State stamps, and Pacific Island maps. Eddie's mother was delighted. She saw great value in such useless activity. "He's a highly intelligent boy who needs to have his mind constantly stimulated," she told her husband.

"It's another part of his body that needs to be stimulated—by a good swift kick from behind," said Joe Maki.

In his spare time, Eddie ignored the usual Coppertown sports of fishing, hunting, skating, skiing, boating, and camping. For exercise, he played the bagpipes his mother had bought him for his birthday and played forward on the high school basketball team.

Still, Eddie sought the respect of his Finnish peers. He had been told all of his life that a real man could keep his family eating well with a steady supply of wild game with or without the permission of the State Department of Natural Resources. He had also been told that a real man could always keep his family warm with a steady supply of wood from his own lot.

Eddie's dad had several wood lots. When Eddie was a junior, Joe Maki hired a Finn named Paavo to cut the pulp wood for the mill in Ontonagon. Eddie became Paavo's assistant. By mid-summer, Eddie could select which trees were ready for cutting. Eddie could drop a tree right where he wanted it, could limb it, peel it, drag it to the road using Paavo's ancient tractor, and could cut it into proper lengths for the mill. He and Paavo together loaded the truck that Paavo leased from the mill.

That summer, after work, Paavo taught Eddie the subtleties of hunting. To Paavo, the hunt was as necessary to his manhood as breathing. By the end of the summer, Paavo had become the first person that Eddie trusted implicitly. For the first time, Eddie felt at least a little bit like a Finn.

Paavo was the ninth son of a Finnish couple with fifteen children. Paavo had grown up poor, eating mostly potatoes. As a boy he had learned to snare rabbits, had graduated to shotgunning partridge and woodcock, and, by thirteen, had regularly poached deer with his older brothers.

When Eddie returned to school for his senior year, he often met Paavo on Saturday nights at the dances at the Finnish Miners' Union Hall. Paavo was twenty and very recently married. He and Eddie sat outside in the parking lot on the hood of Paavo's Dodge pick-up and listened to the polka music from inside. The one-man band was Jorma Pavilainen on the accordion. Eddie and Paavo could see, through the open door, the

Finnish girls twirling in circles.

❖   ❖   ❖   ❖   ❖

Every November, the camps along Lake Superior filled with downstate hunters. The hunters hailed from places like Detroit and Lansing, and they had no intention of actually hunting. They had no knowledge of the country and no bait stands. They stayed up late, playing cards with cronies and drinking beer. In the morning, they were hung over. Most stayed in bed until late. A few donned orange garb and walked up and down some nearby country road, rifle ready, hoping a deer would pop out of the woods and stand in the middle of the road long enough for them to shoot it.

By noon, the downstaters had gathered at Coppertown grocery stores to buy loaves of white bread, cans of B&M beans, Vollwerth's hot dogs, hamburger, and cases of Stroh's. Eddie, Paavo and other locals gathered to stare at these phony hunters and to admire their shiny new cars. The locals called the hunters flatlanders and trolls, derogatory terms for anyone living south of the Mackinac Bridge. Eddie and the others exclaimed over the downstaters' stupidity. "Dumb bastards can't tell a cow from a deer," said Paavo, voicing the town's clichéd wisdom.

That November, Paavo was working in the woods with his brothers and father. He had recently bought a new chain saw and dreamed of buying his own pulp truck. "The damned things are incredibly expensive," he told Eddie. That fall, Paavo had a chance to buy a second-hand truck from one of the paper companies, but he needed a substantial amount of cash down. That was one reason he poached deer nearly every night. He sold the deer to the downstaters for more money than he could earn in the woods. The downstaters were delighted to be able to return to Detroit or Grand Rapids with a trophy. "Poaching is my hobby," Paavo said. "I'd do it even if those damned fools didn't pay me. I guess it's the thrill of the hunt. I don't mean the hunt for the deer. That part's easy. I mean the warden's hunt for me. I like breaking the law. I like being the quarry. It makes me feel good."

On Saturday, Paavo asked Eddie to join him for a poaching spree since his usual poaching partner, Onni Koski, was unavailable. "That damned Onni had to take his wife to Green Bay to visit her folks. Imagine!

Right in the middle of the hunting season! I've got several contracts for deer," Paavo said, sucking at a bottle of Stroh's and pushing his straight blonde hair out of his eyes. "We'll have to hit the dirt roads tonight."

Dirt roads in northern Michigan led to abandoned farms whose owners had fled the land generations before. The farmhouses were cellar holes; the fields were abandoned to goldenrod, alder, and saplings. On a crisp late night, Paavo and Eddie drove slowly in Paavo's pickup along these roads. They sipped from water glasses filled with Jim Beam. They stared at the jumping beam of the headlights as the pickup bounced across ruts. Paavo knew the location of every dying orchard along those roads. At the appropriate spot, he brought the pickup to a stop, unrolled his window and flashed his poaching light across a field. The powerful beam picked up the frozen eyes of each deer. "Take the third one," said Paavo, holding the light on a single pair of star-bright eyes. "It's the buck. We can get two hundred for him."

From the passenger side, Eddie leaned across Paavo and rested the barrel of the Browning .30-.30 on the window ledge. Sharp, frigid air blew across Eddie's face and rustled his hair. Eddie aimed below and behind the eyes, imagining in the darkness where the heart beat wildly. Eddie squeezed the trigger. The truck cab exploded with sound, and the deer eyes blinked out. "It's down," exclaimed Paavo, his foot already engaging the clutch. The truck leaped forward and rushed down the road, leaving a funnel of dust behind.

"What time is it?" asked Paavo, rolling up the window and smiling to himself, his blue eyes glowing excitedly. A splash of Jim Beam darkened the crotch of his jeans.

"Eleven," Eddie answered.

They followed a torturous route back to Paavo's place near pit number nine. The house was one of the many company houses built cheaply and in rows before World War I. Pit number nine had stopped working in the thirties, and Paavo's home was surrounded by rusting machinery. Behind it stood a gray and lifeless tailing heap. In Paavo's living room, Paavo and Eddie sat on the worn-out, second-hand couch and watched Johnny Carson on the small black-and-white TV. They ate burgers prepared by Paavo's wife, Donna, and then listened to country music from faraway Chicago. As they sipped more Jim Beam, Paavo told Eddie about the time he shot a moose when he was clearing timber off leased land in Canada. "I didn't have a knife with me," he said, grinning fiendishly. "I had to use the chain saw to gut and quarter it. Jesus, what a mess! Then I carried the quarters to the pickup, covered them with a tarp and drove right across the border. Me and the old lady ate moose all winter. Tastes like horse—deep red and grainy but good."

Eddie remembered fondly that that was the kind of story Paavo often told.

At two a.m., Paavo announced it was time to go get the deer. He and Eddie climbed into the pickup and drove back to the field off the dirt road. They parked in a secluded turn-off under a towering oak. They were both quite drunk, but the frigid air sobered them fast as they worked their way out into the field without the aid of a flashlight. Several times, Eddie stumbled over tussocks, and once he stepped up to his knee into a hole filled with icy water. Paavo laughed. "Fucking amateur!" he exclaimed.

Paavo had an uncanny sense of direction and distance. Maybe it came with practice. He led Eddie right to the carcass. The deer was still warm. "Damned good shot!" exclaimed Paavo, and, in the darkness, he gave a thumbs-up. Eddie warmed with pride. Paavo bent over and stuck his finger in the small, neat hole where the bullet had entered. "You broke his neck," he said.

Paavo pulled out his *puukko*, the Finnish knife he had honed to razor sharpness. Paavo worked quickly and deftly. Along the deer's abdomen, his blade sliced a thin line that soon widened into a rent, and then into a huge hole ballooning with guts. A powerful odor filled the air. The smell reminded Eddie of the forest—of the rank smell of a swamp mixed with the ripe decay of fallen acorns, ferns, and sedge grass. Paavo completed his cut, reached his full arm with knife deep inside and behind the smoking entrails. With a few swift movements, he detached the entire mass and, with both arms, swept the entrails into a hissing pile beside the carcass. On his knees, Paavo bent forward and wiped his arms and knife on a tuffet of brown hay and goldenrod. "Damn! I should've brought a rag!" he cried. "I smell so strong that a warden will know from a hundred yards that I just gutted a deer! Let's hope we don't get stopped!"

When he was relatively clean, Paavo and Eddie each grabbed a rear leg of the deer and dragged it, running, back to the truck. When they reached it, they were afraid to pause. Even at that crazy hour, a warden might be prowling. They each grabbed an end and heaved the deer over the sideboard into the truck bed. Quickly, Paavo climbed into the bed and secured a tarp over the animal. Then he leaped to the ground. He and Eddie jumped into the cab, secured the water glasses full of Jim Beam that they'd left earlier on the cab floor, and they sped away. The hot blood smell rose from Paavo's arms and permeated the cab. The smell burned Eddie's nostrils.

"Goddamn, boy, that's a good one. Six points. I'll go around to the camps tomorrow. Some asshole from Detroit may give me two and a half. We'll have good drinking tomorrow. And Donna wants a new hi-fi. Things are going good. Onni and I got two others just two nights ago. Sold 'em for three hundred. Had to split that with Onni." Paavo was jubilant. He gulped down the Jim Beam and refilled his glass from the half gallon on the cab floor.

Paavo pulled up at Eddie's home. "Maybe we can go again next weekend," Paavo suggested. "I've got to work between now and then. I'm logging some camp lots near Misery Bay."

"Maybe," Eddie said as he climbed heavily down from the cab. He felt tired to the bones, and a sharp, steady ache sat somewhere just behind his eyes. He already dreaded the hangover of the following day.

"I'll let you have fifty for tonight's work," Paavo said. He reached over, slammed the door and sped away.

Eddie staggered into his parents' home and climbed the stairs to his bedroom. He felt worn out, as if essential parts of himself were ready to snap. He hated the feeling.

A couple of days later, Paavo drove past Eddie as he walked home from basketball practice. Paavo pulled over and waited. Eddie climbed into the cab, shoved his athletic bag under the dash. Paavo handed him two twenties and a ten. "Do you want to go out again tonight?" he asked.

Eddie didn't want to hurt Paavo's feelings, but he needed to be truthful. Besides, he and Paavo had always understood each other. "I can't," Eddie said. "I've got to keep in shape for basketball. Plus next fall I want to play for the university."

"Of course," said Paavo. "I understand. Guys like you are never serious poachers. You do it once just for the experience and for the proof that you're a regular guy. Well, at least you've now had the experience, and Onni should be back on Sunday."

"It's not my idea of fun," Eddie explained. "Getting drunk, cold, wet, and exhausted just isn't a terrific time. I felt horrible the next day."

"Don't worry about it," laughed Paavo. "You were okay. You're a steady shot, and you weren't scared. Next summer, I'll need someone to help me load the truck. I could get that damned fool Jason Latvis. He works like a son of a bitch as long as I put a cold beer on the truck hood in plain sight and tell him he can have it as soon as we're done. The problem is that he's incredibly stupid. I have to tell him how to do every little thing or he'll screw it up. So, do you want to be my loader? If you're going to college, you'll need the money. I'll pay a regular wage."

"You're going to lease the truck!"

"Yep."

"That's great," Eddie exclaimed.

✿   ✿   ✿   ✿   ✿

For the remainder of his senior year, Eddie dabbled with the idea of going to college to study something totally impractical and totally non-Finnish—something that he knew his mother would approve of but that would horrify his father and all the Finns in town. He thought of studying poetry at the Naropa Institute in Colorado. He thought of studying Tibetan at Indiana University or Basque culture in Reno. His father announced that he would not spend one dime on such foolishness.

In the end, Eddie decided to become the one kind of official that all of the Finnish men in his hometown would have to respect. Eddie went to Michigan State University to study Wildlife Management. When he returned to the Keweenaw Peninsula five years later, he was a game warden for the DNR. Paavo was astounded but not too worried. Paavo had given up poaching and made a lot more money by growing pot on the lots he cleared. Eddie's dad was very proud of his son. So were all the other Finns. Or at least that's what they said. But the night Eddie jailed Onni Koski for poaching, he wondered how they would react. He found out a few days later when he overheard a couple of well-known senior-citizen poachers in a coffee shop. "Young Maki will be a good warden," one of the old men said from the next booth. "He's smart, and he'll be fair. If he catches us, we'll know where we stand."

"*If* he catches us," said the other old guy, laughing. "He's not that smart yet."

Eddie smiled. He had finally found his place in the community, and he had their respect. He felt he was home at last. "I'm a Finn after all," he said to himself. "For a while there, I just wasn't aware of it."

Heikki Heikkinen

Hunting Deer

Heikki was a neighbor and a friend who, except for a stint in the army, had lived all of his life in the Upper Peninsula. In his eighty-some years, he had developed his own way of doing things and his own view of life. A dedicated outdoors man, he didn't take too kindly to his body letting him down as he aged. But, as so often happens as people gather years, his sight began to fail. Finally, he was forced to wear bifocals, which always seemed to hang at the end of his nose. Often he bobbed his head up and down, one moment peering over the glasses at the person to whom he spoke, another moment peering through the top of the glasses at something far away, and the next moment lifting his head ridiculously to peer through the bottom lens at something close up.

The glasses, however, did not prevent him from seeing himself as a kind of Finnish Natty Bumppo every fall.

At the beginning of the hunting season, Heikki made his annual hunting trip to the Holiday gas station to buy a license and shells and to purchase a truckload of moldy carrots, half-rotten potatoes, and badly bruised apples. Heikki dumped the foodstuffs under an apple tree behind his sauna and hoped the deer would find it.

He used to dump the deer bait in sight of his kitchen window, under a different apple tree not far from the house. The deer always found it. He'd wait for sunrise on opening day in the warm, darkened kitchen. He'd sip coffee by the potful and peer through that partially opened kitchen window with his rifle resting on the ledge. When the sun rose and he could make out the deer, he would choose the largest and blast away.

Heikki switched to putting the bait near the sauna window because the distance was less. Even then, he worried that he wouldn't be able to see. He put an extra powerful scope on his rifle. He said it made the deer look as huge and fierce as Godzilla. But he was afraid that with the bifocals he would see two deer where there was one, and he wouldn't know which was real.

Heikki was also worried that, if he shot a big buck, he would get excited, forget himself and run outside in the buff to see his trophy. Plus his neighbor, Hilda Maki, had those binoculars.

I told him I didn't understand.

"There's no way I'll wait in an unheated sauna in the cold before dawn," said Heikki. "I'll be taking a sauna while I wait. I'll be hunting in my natural state."

"But won't the hot sauna steam up your scope?" I asked.

Heikki hadn't thought of that. Then he was doubly worried.

Heikki used to be a real hunter—every bit as daring as Frank Buck or Ernest Hemingway. When he was younger, he would dump the deer bait in his back field. Then he'd wait in a blind constructed from an old picnic table. He'd even wear the appropriate orange jacket and an orange hat with ear lappers.

But in his old age, Heikki found that kind of adventure too much. "My bones get stiff, my coffee gets cold, my nose runs, and my hand shakes," he said.

This could be one of the last years Heikki hunts. "It's getting too much for me," he said sadly. "The sporting life is for younger men."

In the meantime, I waited for opening day, knowing that Heikki couldn't chew steak with his false teeth. He would disperse the venison among his friends, including me. He would probably bring me a couple of roasts too. Eating that venison would make me feel like a man's man. None of that chicken meat for me! I would soon be eating North American big game! Daniel Boone, watch out!

Old Finnish Cooking

Old Heikki was an old-fashioned Finn with old-fashioned tastes in food. He liked to eat the kinds of food his grandparents ate in Finland. His homemade *viili* was stringy but rich and creamy, far superior to Dannon. He ate his home-pickled fish right out of the jar with his fingers and didn't understand why his chic granddaughter served store-bought pickled herring in cream sauce on a platter with a toothpick stuck in each piece. "A toothpick is only useful with peanut brittle," he said.

Heikki's idea of a good American meal was canned and frozen in the forties and fifties. He preferred beef to other meats and liked it fried or roasted. He liked to fry his steak in butter to a crisp, even, dark color on the outside and dry gray inside. A properly cooked roast, according to Heikki, shrank to about a quarter of its size raw. A thick slice from a Heikki-cooked roast sat heavy and gray on the plate, like a chunk of cinder block.

Two ingredients were usually essential when Heikki cooked American—cream of mushroom soup and Jell-O. He stirred the soup into all leftovers and called it a casserole. He added a can of mixed fruit to the Jell-O. For a Finnish touch, he mixed dill into both.

Heikki liked to fry his porkchops and chicken in a thick flour batter so the grease from the meat along with the grease in the pan soaked into the batter for extra flavor. He liked to wash the grease down with a big glass of buttermilk.

Heikki was not an okra or kohlrabi kind of guy. Artichokes totally baffled him. He didn't know if they were a fruit or a kind of thorn bush. He knew his Italian neighbors ate them, but he didn't know how or why.

He stuck to root vegetables, like turnips, rutabagas, carrots, and beets, but sometimes he would eat corn, green beans, cabbage, or peas. Other vegetables did not exist in Heikki's world.

The proper way to cook a vegetable, said Heikki, was for a long time in a lot of water. Then he drained it and greased it up with thick slabs of butter and sprinkled it liberally with salt and pepper.

Today there are crazy people out there who spice their foods with garlic and hot pepper, and a whole slough of other condiments. Heikki thought these people should not be allowed across the Mackinac Bridge.

Heikki was a real fanatic about potatoes. He liked them with nearly every meal. He preferred the red ones. Rice was for sissies and the hordes of Asia, he said. Pasta was for people who never quite became real Americans.

One summer, one of Heikki's adult grandchildren helped to plant his garden. The grandchild put in snow peas instead of the old-fashioned kind. Heikki was upset.The grandchild told Heikki that he could eat them shell and all, but Heikki couldn't imagine it. "The shells are for pigs and chickens and compost," he said. He shelled a bushel of them and barely had enough peas for one meal.

Some of Heikki's relatives spent awhile in New Hampshire and became addicted to shellfish. They were always trying to get Heikki to eat it, but he refused. He called shrimp "saltwater bugs" and crab "saltwater spiders." He insisted that lobster was a form of scorpion. He knew all about scorpions, having stepped on one at the base in Texas when he was in the service.

Those same relatives also tried to change Heikki's drinking habits. His grandson took him over to a restaurant in Houghton that boasted one hundred and one brands of beer and a lot of mixed drinks with names like "Raspberry Delight" and "The Green Hornet." Heikki ordered his usual Old Milwaukee. They didn't have any. Heikki left in disgust and went to the Monte Carlo, where Old Milwaukee was what they had.

Last Thanksgiving, Heikki's daughter-in-law made a turkey stuffing with orzo, spinach, and oysters instead of stale bread. Heikki examined the stuff during the grace and announced that oysters were no different from big gobs of snot. No one was very hungry after that, so Heikki said it again, only louder. Then Heikki ate a turkey leg and a thigh, and, when no one had touched the other leg and thigh, he ate those too.

For his last birthday, Heikki's nephew from Lansing bought him a fancy grill with a cover. To entice Heikki to use it, the nephew gave Heikki a big thigh from a turkey the nephew had grilled the previous day. A few days later, Heikki decided to give the grill a try. He bought a cheap, ten-pound, parts-missing turkey at Jim's in Houghton. He wasn't sure how the grill worked, and he didn't trust the infernal machine, but he was determined to duplicate his nephew's tasty sample. He knew a well-done turkey took a long time. He decided to start the cooking at midnight, so it would be done for the following day's dinner.

Heikki put the turkey in its usual roasting pan and salted it down. Then he poured a big pile of coals into the grill and thoroughly soaked the pile with kerosene. To make sure it would light, he followed the kerosene with a squirt or two of gasoline. Then he lit a twisted piece of newspaper and, from a respectable distance, tossed the flaming paper in the general direction of the grill. With a loud boom, the coals exploded into a ball of flame five feet high.

After the flames subsided, Heikki added a lot more coals and placed the roasting pan with the turkey on the grill. He put on the top, opened the air vent and went to bed.

The next morning, Heikki added more coals.

At noon, he added a few more. His twenty-pound bag was almost empty.

He checked the roasting turkey about three o'clock in the afternoon. It had been cooking for about fifteen hours. He was surprised to find it was definitely done.

I asked Heikki how it was.

It was very dry, he said. He had to chew for a long time. It resembled jerky, he said, but had a permanence that jerky lacked.

Heikki blamed the grill. After it cooled, he disassembled it and took it (and most of the turkey) to the county landfill. The grill now rests there in peace, not disturbing the eating habits of anyone else.

In recent years, younger members of Heikki's family tried to introduce him to modern American cooking. As a Christmas present, a nephew bought him a fondue pot. Another bought him an electric wok. Heikki never took either out of its box.

Heikki was afraid that he would get all sorts of useless cooking devices as gifts every Christmas. He might be right. I saw a niece of his looking for a crepe maker in K-Mart. She had already bought him a jar of grape leaves at the Keweenaw Co-op. Another relative planned to get him a cookbook with five hundred tofu recipes.

It looked as if Heikki's eating habits were under siege. Heikki was not too worried though. He said they would never change his tastes in food. "Even if it's good," he said, "I'm not going to like it!" He had *sisu*.

Once he asked me over to share his meal of Van Camp's pork and beans with fried Spam and Vienna sausages on the side. I told him I was busy.

Snowmobiling

Almost daily since the middle of October, my friend Heikki sat for an hour or so on his snowmobile in his backyard, revving the engine and dreaming of speeding over snow. He and his buddies had already planned their first long snowmobile trip of the new season. They planned to meet at the Mosquito Inn in Toivola and toss down a few. Then they would journey to the three bars in South Range, go cross country to Houghton to get pickled eggs at the B and B and meatloaf sandwiches at the Ambassador. After that, they would journey to Lake Linden with stops along the way at watering holes in Hancock, Dollar Bay, and Hubbell. In Dollar Bay and Hubbell, some of the guys would play pool and maybe eat a pizza.

Heikki had been an enthusiastic snowmobiler for many years. He said snowmobiling got him out in the fresh air. He also liked the camaraderie and the noise. He insisted that nature in winter was just too quiet. "It takes the roar of a snowmobile engine and the smell of gasoline to add the right touch," he said.

Heikki especially liked participating in a sport without getting hot and sweaty. "All I have to do is sit," he said proudly. "The snowmachine does all the work." Heikki considered this ideal. "If I want to sweat, I'll take a sauna!" he said. He didn't understand why some people preferred to slide across fields on long sticks tied to their boots.

Heikki also insisted that snowmobiling was healthy because it kept him out of the bar. I pointed out to Heikki that he planned to visit nine bars on his first trip, but he insisted that proved his point. "Otherwise, I'd be at the Monte Carlo all night," he said.

Heikki's other winter sports were ice fishing, scooping snow and watching the ski jumping in Ishpeming. Heikki liked to sit on a chair in his fish house with a line in the hole and a case of Old Milwaukee at his feet. He said he didn't care what he caught as long as it wasn't a cold.

He liked scooping snow because it served a purpose—it really irritated his neighbor, Hilda Maki. By spring, Heikki would have a tailing heap of his snow about twelve feet high in Hilda's yard. Heikki called the yearly mounds Mount Heikki. Hilda called them "more of Heikki's devil-ish work," and threatened to call the sheriff if Heikki piled his snow on her property again in the winter.

Heikki really enjoyed watching the ski jumping in Ishpeming. He especially liked to watch from a safe distance in the parking lot on a sunny day when he could sit on the tailboard of his pickup with a case of Old Milwaukee beside him and plenty of pickled fish, pork hocks, and bratwurst to eat.

Heikki said I could come along for the ride when he and his bud-dies gathered at the Mosquito for their snowmobile run. I told him I was not in shape for his kind of rugged outdoor life. Heikki said he was will-ing to get me in shape, starting the next night at the Monte.

I think I'll decline.

Heikki's TV

Heikki's old black-and-white TV finally died. He purchased a new color set complete with remote control and cable hook-up. Heikki admitted that he rarely watched anything except the weather channel. He liked to check on conditions in Duluth, Minnesota, where his son lived, and Helsinki, Finland, where he'd like to be. "It's my connection to the world," he said. He liked to call up his friend Eino and give him the weather conditions in some remote city like Dallas or Cheyenne. Eino had no TV and considered Heikki's meteorological proclamations to be some kind of magic. "How do you know that cowboys in Wyoming are getting wet?" Eino asked.

"You have to take it on faith," said Heikki. "Like going to church."

On his old TV, which only received a fuzzy version of Channel Six from Marquette, Heikki never watched the news. After he bought the new color set, he sometimes did. "To tell you the truth," he said, "I'm sometimes pretty uneducated about things going on in the world. But flipping through the channels with my new remote, I have come across a news station once or twice and have even stopped to listen a few times."

Heikki discovered that the Soviet Union no longer existed. "Boy, was I surprised!" he said. "If it doesn't exist, where are all the people to go?" Heikki feared that all those homeless Soviet citizens would try to sneak into the United States. "This may greatly increase the number of people in other parts of the country," he said. "The jobless rate will increase, prices will skyrocket, and there will be a lot more homeless people from the tundra in New York." Heikki was not too worried about a massive influx of Soviet citizens into the Upper Peninsula, though. "We Finns beat the pants off them in the Winter War," he said, "so they'll stay away from Hancock and Negaunee."

One thing really bothered Heikki. "If the Soviet Union isn't there, who does the president talk to if there is trouble?"

Heikki saw Yeltsin on TV and admitted he didn't like him very much. "He looks like a lot of guys around here who have lived in bars for years. I've met plenty of Yeltsins at the Monte Carlo and the B and B. And that other guy, Gorbachev, had a map on his head."

Heikki saw a news item that said President Clinton was sending a couple of billion dollars to Russia in the form of aid. Heikki wanted to know how that compared to his retirement pension of $686 a month. "First, we beat the pants off them, and now the president wants to give them a new pair!" said Heikki.

Heikki pointed out that a lot of other Copper Country folks agreed with him. "Maybe we should take care of the folks at home first," he said. "Then, after that, we can help the rest of the world."

The Smartass Nephew from Lansing

When Heikki came over for coffee one morning, he was once again fuming over his nephew from Lansing, the smartass who had given him the grill. Heikki's nephew also caught trophy trout with a fly and an itty-bitty line and then threw the fish back in the water. That kind of highbrow fishing enraged Heikki.

For years, Heikki's nephew had a job as a roofer with a construction firm in Lansing. The nephew had two kids and a pregnant wife to support, but he quit the job to return to school. Just before he quit, he took options on a couple of condemned houses in Lansing. The city gave him the houses for nothing with the stipulation that he make the buildings livable once again.

Then the nephew went to one of those government agencies that give home improvement grants to the poor. He was poor since he had quit his job and had no income. The government gave him tens of thousands of dollars to fix up the homes he had gotten for nothing. While the nephew went to school, a couple of free guys from a government retraining program put on new roofs, put in new windows, installed new kitchens, replaced the plumbing and siding, painted and plastered and papered.

Heikki's nephew then sold one of the houses for an obscenely large profit. He and his family moved into the other, which looked brand new. In the meantime, Heikki couldn't afford to get new kitchen cabinets for his wife.

Before he went to school, the nephew went to the financial aid office at his college. Since he had no income, he obtained government grants and low-interest loans to pay for his schooling. The nephew liked the idea of those low-interest loans so much that he borrowed extra money, which he invested at high interest so he could make a considerable profit when he paid the loans back at low interest.

The nephew's pregnant wife went to the welfare office, and the government agreed to cover all her medical expenses. The baby was born premature, with breathing problems. The kid had to spend days in intensive care. The bill to the government was about $100,000. The nephew didn't have to pay a cent, but Heikki needed to take six months to pay back one visit to the emergency room when he had a $150.00 earache.

The nephew earned a college degree, found a better-paying job than he had before, a new home, and a new child—all for free. With the profits from his low-interest loans, he also had a new Bronco.

"So, as a taxpayer, I have about thirty grand invested in my smartass nephew's house," said Heikki. Plus he believed he deserved a share of the profits from the sale of the other house. Taxpayer Heikki also had a considerable investment in his nephew, since taxpayers paid for his schooling. "Plus," said Heikki, "I've got a hundred grand invested in his kid."

Heikki took the totals of state and federal funds donated to his nephew, divided each by the number of taxpayers, and roughly figured his own share. He sent his nephew a bill. He told the nephew to bypass the government and just send his share in cash directly to him. The nephew told Heikki that he was crazy.

"But I'm not the crazy one," said Heikki. "The crazy one is the government!"

In the meantime, the smartass nephew is thinking about quitting his new job and checking out more government giveaway programs. He said it's just too profitable to stop now.

Scanning the News

Recently, Heikki was looking for the weather channel on his new color TV, but the cable company had realigned the channels, and he got a news broadcast by mistake. Heikki found out that Israel and the PLO had made peace. Heikki was surprised. He'd read in his Bible that Israel was always fighting with somebody, but he didn't know they were still at it. "It'll start again," he told me. "Those Bible people are always fighting about one thing or another."

Heikki also found out that American soldiers fought in Somalia. He had never heard of the place. He only owned maps of Finland, the Upper Peninsula, the United States, and the Sturgeon River, where he liked to fish. Somalia wasn't on any of them.

Heikki also head about a new government report that said that the majority of adult Americans were functionally illiterate. Heikki was pretty sure he was among them. He was very proud to be part of such a large group, especially since Finns were such a tiny minority. Heikki was worried, though, that somebody might think he was stupid, so he bought a new coffee cup that said, I'M FROM FINLAND WHAT'S YOUR EXCUSE?

In the local paper, Heikki read about the suicide doctor, Jack Kevorkian. Heikki had a hard time sleeping after that. He kept waking up in the middle of the night, certain that Dr. Kevorkian and his infernal machine were at the foot of the bed. Heikki finally gave up and went out to the kitchen to have a glass of milk and to do the "Word Power" exercises from his wife's latest *Reader's Digest*.

The next day, Heikki decided to try out some of those big words on me. "Dr. Death's a circumstantial murderer," Heikki told me.

I asked Heikki to explain what he meant. "Dr. Death didn't just shoot them," said Heikki. "He got the diseased people who used the good doctor's services to do it themselves."

Heikki insisted that Kevorkian ought to be convicted of murder, locked up, put away, imprisoned, tied up, drawn and quartered. "Then they ought to stuff his head in his own death machine," he added.

I wondered why Heikki hated the doctor so much. "I'm only eighty-five—too young to die," he said. He also objected along religious lines. "Human misery ought to be dealt with properly," he said. "Misery is God's department." Heikki added that Dr. Kevorkian went against "the Bible's version of murder because he expedites people."

I asked Heikki if "expedite" was one of the "Word Power" words. It was. I told Heikki that the people who committed suicide were very sick—without hope of recovery. "Maybe suicide was good for them," I said.

Heikki scoffed at that. "When people commit suicide, they ruin their careers, damage their reputations, and put an emotional strain on their family!"

"It's not good for their health either," I added.

Relatives from Florida

Since my friend Heikki had never been anywhere, he knew with absolute certainty that the Copper Country was the only place to live. I'm exaggerating a little, of course. Heikki's been to Green Bay a couple of times on shopping trips. He hated Green Bay and called it toilet town, referring to a common product of the local paper mill. When he was there, Heikki worried every second that he would get lost and never find the ribbon of highway that led back to Iron Mountain and the salvation of home.

One thing Heikki liked about Green Bay was the coffee shop in Port Plaza Mall. While his wife shopped, Heikki bought a cup of steaming java, found an empty seat at one of the benches in the center of an intersection, and sat down to enjoy his styrofoamed coffee and watch the passing crowds. He was amazed that such a huge space was heated. "It must take a lot of wood!" he said.

In Green Bay, Heikki dressed the same as he dressed at home. He wore his red-and-black, checkered wool cap with ear flaps, his torn, frazzled, bleached-out K-Mart flannel shirt, his heavy green wool pants with suspenders, and his swampers. No one else there dressed that way. "They wore really funny-looking clothes," he said, shocked by haircuts of the passing young.

Heikki had many relatives in Lake Worth, Florida, but he hadn't seen them for years and didn't like them when he did. He said they were all snobs. "They talk about their ancestry as if they were the Finnish version of *Gone with the Wind*," complained Heikki. "They like to think their ancestors transformed Florida from a 'gater pit into the progressive state that Florida is today—a place full of money-grubbing developers and homicidal maniacs," said Heikki.

But ever since he heard about Hurricane Andrew on the weather channel, Heikki periodically invited his relatives to move to God's Country. One fall, to his shock and chagrin, they took him up on his offer. They arrived with all their personal effects stuffed into their rear-wheel-drive van and their bright red Dodge Daytona sports car. Their furniture soon arrived in a moving van. For a few days they lived with Heikki, drinking up his coffee, dirtying his sauna, and generally interrupting his routine. Then they bought an old farm just down the road and set out to thoroughly enjoy the Copper Country in all its natural glory.

The purchased farmhouse was set back from the road, and the furnace burned wood. Heikki tried to warn his relatives about the work wood furnaces entailed, but they saw the old farm as romantic—as an image off a postcard.

Nearly every day that fall, the ex-Floridians took a walk in the woods, ostensibly to gather wood for the winter. Instead, they listened to the chatter of squirrels, the chirping of birds, and the rustling of the breezes through the trees. Occasionally, they cut up a tree blown down in a storm. They'd use a handsaw because Heikki's chain saw was too noisy and too unnatural. Heikki would transport these wood scraps to the house with his tractor or pickup. He warned them that they needed a lot more wood, but they wouldn't listen. "It can't be that cold," they said.

Nearly every day all fall, they asked Heikki when the first snow would come. They had never had a white Christmas but knew what one looked like from Hallmark cards. Near the end of November, the first snow fell. The Floridians came over to Heikki's place to watch in rapture. They mixed martinis and hoisted the cocktails in toast to the winter wonderland. Heikki was disgusted by their naiveté. He came over to my place and drowned his irritation in bottles of Old Milwaukee. "Those damned fools think they're on a weekend trip to Aspen!" he said. "They don't know about a Copper Country winter, and you can't tell them. They don't listen!"

The second snowfall was about an inch. The ex-Floridians had a wonderful time shoveling it off their driveway and front steps. "This is the life," they said, breathing deeply of the crisp air.

The third storm coated every tree, shrub, and blade of grass with sparkling white lace. The ex-Floridians were so excited that they ran from tree to tree and bush to bush, exclaiming over the beauty and taking pictures with an expensive 35-millimeter camera. About twenty times that day, they called Heikki to tell him what they had seen. He was not impressed and took great delight in the fact that the sun melted all the snow the next day.

After that, the weather stayed mild for several weeks, but, about a week before Christmas, the temperature plummeted to zero, and it began to snow in earnest. In fact, it never stopped snowing for the next two weeks. In one day, fourteen inches fell; on the next, eight more fell, and on the third, another twelve.

The Floridians were outside nearly all of the first day, shoveling the fluffy white stuff and throwing snowballs at each other. Just after they broke through the high bank left by the snowplow and had reached the highway, the plow came by again and buried their work. They decided to give up and go into town for a movie, but their rear-wheel-drive van slid off the road at the first turn. They had to ask Heikki to get them out with his truck and a chain. Then they tried to return home, but the plow had come by and filled in their driveway again. After much shoveling and cursing, they broke through the roadside bank and shoveled enough of the driveway to get the van just barely off the road. Then they plodded through the new accumulation to their home and went inside to sleep. They were too tired to toast the arrival of winter with martinis.

By morning, their furnace was out, and their pipes were frozen. Heikki had told them about getting up in the middle of the night to replenish the wood-burning furnace, but they had not taken him seriously. They put on lots of sweaters and then their new L.L. Bean coats with all the pockets. They got the fire going again and chipped a little ice from the sink and put it in a cup for coffee. The ice had collected because the faucet leaked, and they had not yet fixed it. In fact, that's how they had discovered that their pipes were frozen: the faucet had stopped leaking.

They decided to visit Heikki and drink his coffee. When they opened the front door, a gust of wind nearly blew them over, and a swirl of snow scooted across the room. They had to fight their way out onto the porch, and, for a while, they couldn't find their shovels because they had neglected the night before to stand them up. They were buried a few feet from the house. They made a narrow path out to the road but found that the plow had come by several times during the night, and the growing accumulation of snow had formed a roadside bank that buried the entire rear half of the van. For the next two hours, they shoveled. Once the van was cleared, they got it started, but they had to wait a few minutes for the engine to warm before they dared drive it. In the meantime, the plow came by once again and reburied the van. The temperature gauge on the van was soaring anyway because no one had told them to check their antifreeze.

They braved the cold and wind and walked to Heikki's place. Twice they fell but were not hurt. People in four-wheel-drive trucks sped nonchalantly by, waving cheerily to them. Heikki's yard was more or less clear of snow, the entire mass of white stuff deposited as a small mountain in Hilda Maki's yard. When the Floridians arrived, Hilda was on her porch cursing Heikki and threatening to call the sheriff. Heikki told his relatives to pay Hilda no mind. "She's not very neighborly," he said.

Heikki's relatives looked close to death from freezing. Heikki took them into the warm kitchen, gave them steaming mugs of coffee mixed with a little brandy and waited for them to thaw. When they did, they cursed the plowman for about half an hour and then set out to tell Heikki all the rest of their woes. Heikki didn't want to hear. He explained what they had to do if they were to survive to see their first white Christmas. They'd have to buy a few loads of wood, and they'd have to keep a fire blazing all the time in the uninsulated old farmhouse. They'd have to sell the van and the Daytona and buy a truck with a plow. They'd have to insulate their water lines where they were above ground.

The relatives said they couldn't believe that anyone was stupid enough to live in such a godforsaken region. They said they knew Heikki was dumb, but they never knew how dumb until they tried to live in his part of the country. "If I'm so dumb," he said to them, "how come I'm not the one that's freezing?"

Heikki gave the relatives a ride back to their place, got their van out onto the road, plowed their driveway, scooped the path to the doorway, checked out their furnace until a fire blazed, and thawed their water line and their toilet. All of that took him until supper time. The relatives just watched him work, complained and drank martinis.

That night, the relatives woke up because the furnace had gone out again, and there was no more wood. The waterlines had refrozen, and, at the end of the driveway, the van sat, reburied by the plow several times over. The relatives went berserk. They grabbed an ax and tore into the partition dividing the living room from the dining room, throwing pieces of studding into the furnace to get the fire going again. Then they took a saw to a beam and got some wood that would burn for some time. They went back to bed.

Snow accumulated on the roof all night, and, by morning, the weight of it was too much for the weakened house. Before breakfast, the roof caved in. The cave-in toppled the chimney, and the fire in the furnace broke out into the basement. In a few minutes, the house was an inferno. The relatives ran naked out into the deep snow in the yard and turned to watch their possessions go up in flames.

The husband cursed the anonymous plowman and insisted that he could have made it in the Copper Country if it weren't for that damned plow. Then he and his wife broke into tears and began to shake violently from the cold.

Heikki drove over to see why they had burned down their house. "I hope you had a long sauna before you ran out here buck naked," he said. He gave his relative's wife his jacket but decided to let his relative suffer awhile. Plus he wanted Hilda Maki to get an eyeful through her binoculars from her upstairs bedroom window.

All Heikki could think about was that his relatives would be living with him, and, for a few days, that was true. They crowded his house long enough to have a white Christmas. On New Year's Eve, Heikki took them on a snowmobile jaunt. He drove very fast and dumped them into snowbanks several times. By the sixth watering hole, they were very drunk and very depressed, and Heikki was very happy. He abandoned them under the pool table in the Loading Zone and picked them up early the next morning after they'd slept off about half their hangover.

The next day, they headed south in the new Ford Taurus they had bought with the last of their savings.

"I figure they won't be back," Heikki told me. Still, they had seriously shaken his faith in the superiority of Finns. Before, he had known with certainty that all Finns were born with the Lutheran version of original sin, just like everyone else, but he'd also known that Finns were born with an original knowledge of how to use an ax and a shovel, which gave them one step up on normal humans. He also knew that Finnish was the language of God. He'd realized this when he read in the paper that the oldest Bible in the Copper Country was a Finnish-language one in Jacobsville. He reasoned that all the English versions had to be translated from the oldest one.

Heikki didn't hear from his relatives after they left. He guessed he wouldn't. "With those Michigan plates on their car, they've probably been shot dead in Miami by now," he said.

Bird's-eye Maple

For many years, Heikki searched for his own version of the Holy Grail. For Heikki, the most precious of religious artifacts was a bird's-eye maple. "If I could find just one, it'd be worth forty or fifty thousand dollars," said Heikki. Sometimes Heikki dreamed he leased for the cutting forty acres somewhere in the back of beyond, and the entire forty turned out to be covered with dozens and dozens of bird's-eye maples. "That would be heaven," he said. When he thought about it, he began to dance a little *raatikka* all by himself, with some invisible woman (presumably not his wife) twirling at his side.

A few months ago, Heikki leased a forty for the cutting somewhere out by Winona, which is the Copper Country's version of the back of beyond. He was too old to clear a lot, but he thought he'd run out there and take core samplings of all the good-sized maples—just to see if a bird's-eye maple were among them. He took the lease with him and referred frequently to its facts and figures, but his eyes were pretty bad, and his sense of direction wasn't so great either. He never found that damned forty.

This winter he went searching for it again—this time by snowmobile. He got lost and almost froze before he found his way back to the Mosquito Inn, where he warmed up with the help of one ice-cold Old Milwaukee after another. Finally, about a week later, he gave up the search and transferred the lease. "Now somebody else will get all that bird's-eye maple for sure," he said.

To overcome his frustration and to get back a little self-respect, Heikki decided to learn a new word from the "Word Power" list in his wife's latest *Reader's Digest*. He chose "schizophrenic" and was astounded at how well it described himself. "I'm a schizophrenic kind of guy," he told me, heavily accenting the first syllable. "I have a split personality. A voice inside tells me to do one thing, and I usually do just the opposite," he said. The voice inside him speaks Finnish and sounds a lot like his mother. "But she's been dead for forty years, and that doesn't make a lot of sense," he said.

Heikki gave me some examples of his own split personality. "For one thing, I married a woman who keeps a neat house and goes to church to pray for me," he said. "Plus she talks all the time, and I can be silent for days at a time as long as I'm sober."

Heikki also couldn't bear to throw anything away that might one day be useful. He was tight that way. That's why he had an ugly pile of old tires in his front yard and the skeletons of half a dozen old cars in his back pasture. At the same time, though, he planted flowers in the tires and hid the cars behind some lilac bushes.

He could also be tight with money. He often stretched a piece of meat through at least three meals in the form of a roast, soup, and a casserole. But, if he started drinking on Friday afternoon, he had no idea where his check went by Monday morning.

Heikki was not too worried about any of this. Mostly he only worried that someone else would find the mythic forty full of bird's-eye maple. He checked the local paper, the *Finnish American Reporter*, and the weather channel daily to see if such a find had been mentioned. He listened with a keen ear to the conversations in local bars. He hadn't heard anything that indicated that other people were looking for the same treasure lode. "As long as they don't know about it, my chances of being the one to make the find are greatly improved," reasoned Heikki. Whenever he heard two guys at the Monte Carlo talking about bird's-eye maple, he tried to turn the conversation away from trees and towards frozen vegetables. His ploy seemed to work since no one at the Monte Carlo had suddenly showed signs of great wealth. "One of these days they're going to refer to me as the bird's-eye king," said Heikki. "I'll have so much dough that they'll name a hockey rink or a ski jump after me."

Heikki had always wanted a world-class ski jump in Hancock, preferably right behind his house so he could watch through a window from the warmth of his kitchen. He would invite the great Finnish jumpers to compete locally—Nykanen, Nieminen, and Ahonen. Plus all of them would fit right in at the Monte Carlo. "I hear they like a nip or two," said Heikki.

Heikki did not approve of the new V-style jumping much in vogue. He preferred the windmill method. He especially preferred the old days, when Ishpeming iron miners would be out with the guys on Saturday night and would set a new North American record jumping at Suicide Hill on Sunday afternoon, then be back in the mines on Monday morning. "They were real men," said Heikki, who scoffed at the jumpers who competed at Lillehammer. Heikki hated their form-fitting, brightly colored, silky-sissy outfits all covered with ads. "They might as well jump wearing a Nancy Kerrigan skirt," said Heikki.

Heikki had fond memories of the great jumpers of the past, such as Rudy Maki, Coy Hill, and the Bietila brothers. Decades before, Heikki owned a camp near the Bietilas'. "They were good old boys," he said fondly, remembering cold dips in the lake, saunas, speakers in the jack pines broadcasting Detroit Tigers games, and horseshoes going *clink clink*. "They were the kinds of guys who could do handstands on a tree limb and pole vault with a cigarette in the mouth," said Heikki. He insisted they weren't afraid of anything. "When you come off that chute, you either jump to clear a piece of earth or you reach for the sky and try to fly. Most are afraid to fly, but those guys weren't. They were the original flying Finns."

Tears filled Heikki's eyes when he talked about the old days, but there was a lot of pride in his eyes, too. Clearly, he saw himself, who never leaped higher than the running board of his pickup, as equally fearless. He had never reached for the sky but might hold a world's record for reaching for an Old Milwaukee. He dreamed of great things but, considering his advanced age, was running out of time.

"One bird's-eye will do," said Heikki. "I'd be set for life."

He planned on sneaking over to Hilda Maki's and taking core samples of the maples in her front yard. The search went on.

Losing Faith in the Weather Channel

Heikki hadn't been to church for seventy-two of his eighty-some years, but he retained a child's faith in a Lutheran God. He made up for his nonattendance at church by faithfully watching Carl Pellonpaa's *Finland Calling* every Sunday morning on Channel Six. He also attended numerous church breakfasts and suppers, stuffing himself on sacramental sausages and potluck casseroles. Plus he prayed a lot when the fish weren't biting on Portage Lake.

Until one winter's long stretch of extreme cold, Heikki also had a child's faith in science. Then he was not so sure and suffered a kind of crisis of faith. The crisis began with a series of incorrect forecasts on the weather channel. "They'd say it was fifteen below zero in Hancock, but I'd check my own thermometer, and it would be more like twenty-two below," Heikki told me. "They were almost never right." He soon noticed that the long-range forecast was always changing, too. On Sunday, the weather girl would say that by Wednesday it would be twenty-five below, but, by Tuesday, she would have revised her forecast downward. That's when Heikki began seriously questioning the laws of science. Ever since he got cable, he had taken great pleasure memorizing the world's temperatures and weather off the weather channel, and he enjoyed calling his friend Eino every day to tell him it was sunny and eighty-five degrees in Honolulu or rainy and sixty-one in Birmingham, England. But with the weather girl giving the wrong temperatures even for Hancock, Heikki was silenced. "I don't believe any of that crap anymore," he said.

He questioned what life was all about. "If you can't trust the weather channel, what can you trust?" he asked.

This winter, Heikki's pipes froze and refroze almost as fast as he could thaw them. Again and again, he struggled with a salamander down in the basement. The salamander was a machine that blasted a stream of hot air at frozen pipes, but Heikki's burned kerosene, and the odor nauseated him. The smell permeated Heikki's home. Then his toilet line froze, and the waste accumulated in his basement for more than a week before he smelled the problem.

Heikki was so despondent that he couldn't sleep. He didn't even get undressed for bed. He sat in his darkened kitchen until three a.m. — listening for the freezing of his pipes. He stared out the kitchen window at the seemingly endless mounds of snow. He could feel the sub-zero cold creeping into the kitchen through even the tiniest of cracks under the door and around the window sill. He felt the emptiness of existence. At one point, he pulled the family Bible off the shelf, blew the dust off the cover, and opened it for the first time since 1922. Unfortunately, he had opened it randomly to a whole page of begats. He tried to find meaning in who had begat whom, but he soon gave up and put the book away.

He turned on the TV and flipped through the channels. He stopped at one of the religious channels and stared in wonder for a while. The channel horrified him. He turned off the TV, put on his big orange hunting jacket that bulged with down, pulled his opossum-fur hat tightly over his ears, stepped into his unlaced swampers, went out to his truck, and got it started in spite of the cold. He drove to the Citgo that stayed open twenty-four hours a day. He filled up his gas tank at the pump and then went inside. The girl behind the counter was half asleep. "What's it all mean?" Heikki shouted at her.

The girl was suddenly alert. She stared at Heikki with round and baffled eyes.

"You can't trust anyone anymore," he said. "Not even the guy on the weather channel. So, what's it all mean?"

Without a word, the girl reached over and handed Heikki the money from the cash register.

Heikki stared at the money for a moment, took in the fright in the girl's eyes, and then gave her back the money. He assured her that he had not come to rob the place. "The only one who gets robbed at this place is me," he said, referring to the price of gas. He remembered when it had been fifteen cents a gallon.

Heikki told the girl he had just been watching the religious channel on TV. "Those people have about fifteen yards of snow-white hair," he said. "They pile all of it up on their heads and blow dry it so it puffs out. It looks like their heads are stuck in pillows," he added. He went on to tell the girl about the number at the bottom of the screen. "Every half minute, they ask for money," he said. "It's disgusting!" He told the girl how one preacher went on and on about the Book of Revelations, Judgment Day, and the end of the world. "He sounded really happy about it! He sounded like he was waiting gleefully for it to happen. He said the Angel Gabriel was going to come down and pick up people like him and take them to heaven, while old Heikki gets left behind, trying to thaw his freezing pipes for eternity!"

The girl behind the counter didn't say anything. She began to eat a peanut butter cup.

"I don't know what to do," Heikki explained to her. "I've lost my faith in science due to the inaccurate weather reports, and I can't believe in religion because of those crazy TV preachers. Where's Carl Pellonpaa when you really need him?"

After that, Heikki paid for his gas, muttered something about losing faith in the economy and government too, and went out. He got back in his truck and drove over to my place to roust me out of bed and tell me about his encounter with the girl at the Citgo station and about all his other problems. It was four-thirty a.m. I stayed up with him until about six, and then he left, and I went back to bed for a couple of hours.

That evening, I called to see how he was. He said he was fine— that his depression was just an acute case of cabin fever brought on by the cold weather and the deep frost. Apparently, he visited the Monte Carlo after he left me that morning. Then he went to the Mosquito Inn, the Pub in South Range, Partanen's in Dollar Bay, the Loading Zone in Hubbell, and then back to the Monte Carlo. He and his buddies were going to ride their snowmobiles up Brockway Mountain. Heikki insisted that life was looking up.

I asked him if he had regained his faith. He assured me that he had. "I'll be right back at the Lutheran church the next time they have a pancake breakfast," he said with conviction.

"What about the weather channel?" I asked.

"The weather channel is too important a part of my life for me to give it up so easily," Heikki said. He decided that they're sometimes inaccurate just to test his faith. "They don't have to be right every time. Besides, even God once made a mistake."

"And what was that?" I asked.

"He didn't make everyone in the world a Finn," Heikki said.

Fishing

Smelting season arrived in the Copper Country. Heikki brought me several dozen freshly cleaned smelt for breakfast. He and I ate them rolled in corn meal and fried crisp. Between bites, Heikki recited the current temperatures in Mexican resorts. Except for watching the weather channel, smelting was Heikki's favorite sport. He liked getting wet, cold, dirty, smelly, drunk, and tired all in the same night. He numbered these as the sport's redemptive qualities. The lack of a hangover the next day was also an incentive. "Maybe it's because I always fall in a couple of times," said Heikki. "That water is like ice and freezes the alcohol."

Heikki watched fishing shows on PASS and Channel Six from Marquette. He was horrified that the fishermen on those shows always released their catch. Heikki saw no sense in that. "If it's big enough to catch, it's big enough to eat," he said.

Heikki's usual method of fishing was from the back of a boat. He could sit comatose from dawn to dark as long as he had a line in the water. Heikki liked fishing because he could turn off his brain and his mouth while doing it. He reached a kind of zen state or maybe nirvana. "I talk only to the fish," he said. "I urge it to bite my hook."

Heikki had only disdain for sports that required jumping, running, and catching a ball. "Even if you catch it, you can't eat it," he said.

The names of teams confused Heikki. "Why do the prim and proper Mormons call their team the Jazz?" he asked. He wondered why most of the Celtics were black if a Celt was Irish. He wondered why the Mets were from New York if they played all their home games in New Jersey. Heikki said the Buffalo Bisons were redundant.

Sometimes Heikki had no problem with the names. The Braves moved from Boston to Milwaukee to Atlanta because Indians were

54

nomadic, he said. The baseball team from Los Angeles was the Dodgers, he said, because they were always dodging rocks from rioters and bullets from drive-by shootings.

Heikki was baffled, however, that Los Angeles had named its basketball team after his favorite kind of trout. "I could understand calling them Lakers if they had a lake. But it's all desert out there."

The Lakers inspired Heikki to create his own brand of word play. "I caught this Kareem Abdul Jabbar at the head of Keweenaw Bay," he told me one day, showing me a very large laker. He didn't like to fish Torch Lake anymore because, he said, all the fish there were Magic Johnsons.

Heikki planned to put his boat in the water this week. He was excited about the new fishing season. I wouldn't see much of him until fall unless I joined him out there on the water. The problem was that I didn't know how to put my brain into neutral and let it idle. Heikki said I'll never be a fisherman because I think and talk too much.

Maybe he was right. I guess I won't see much of him or his kind until fall.

The New Wal-Mart

Heikki was excited to hear that Wal-Mart was coming to the Copper Country. He had heard that their flannel shirts and antifreeze were cheaper than K-Mart's. Then he found out that Wal-Mart hired senior citizens as greeters, and he decided to apply. His last salaried job was in a CCC camp during the Depression.

Heikki got a tentative offer to be a greeter, but first he had to get rid of the yellow-and-black, checkered K-Mart flannel shirt with the torn elbows, the red spandex suspenders, and the green wool pants with the button-up fly that he ordered from Sears in 1947. He also had to replace his swampers, get a proper haircut, and learn to speak a reasonable facsimile of schoolbook English. Heikki figured all of that would cost him more than the job was worth.

Heikki went to the grand opening anyway—as a spectator. He had heard that Wal-Mart employees had their own national anthem, and he wanted to hear it. A color guard of national guardsmen was there with the state and national flags. Heikki took along a Finnish flag and waved it from the sidelines. The weather channel had said it was going to be a cold and windy day, and, for once, they were right. The pompom girls from local high schools had goose bumps the size of partridge eggs on the back of their legs. Heikki couldn't keep his eyes off those bare legs. The goose bumps, in particular, fascinated him. He couldn't believe anyone was dumb enough to be barelegged when the wind was blowing a gale and it was threatening snow. Five of the girls noticed Heikki staring and approached a deputy of the Houghton County Sheriff's Department. Heikki was accused of sexual harassment and escorted from the premises. Heikki was irate. "I guess they think they have the right to show off their legs in front of a crowd, but I don't have the right to look!" said

Heikki, who had previously heard of *sex* but not **harassment**.

Heikki went home and watched the Tigers play the Rangers in Texas. The wind in Texas was blowing so hard that the pitcher was occasionally blown off the mound. A high pop-up between third base and shortstop ended up misplayed by the first baseman near the first-base line. In the sixth inning, debris from outside the stadium began to blow across the field, and the batter and catcher were temporarily blinded by flying dirt. The game was then suspended.

Heikki was not impressed. He said that today's high-priced ball players lacked *sisu*. He remembered pickup games at the Copper Country diamonds in the first quarter of the century when the wind blowing out of center field would pin the ball to the bat. Back then there used to be a stream that, in the early spring, often overflowed just behind the outfield of the Toivola diamond. During the smelt run, fish would get lost and veer off into the runlets between the clumps of outfield grass. Heikki said he often netted smelt while he waited for someone to hit a fly ball. Then he'd catch the ball with the same net. "Catching a ball with a smelt net is a lot easier than catching one with a glove," he said. "Plus on a really cold day, it doesn't sting the hand."

Heikki was thinking of writing the baseball commissioner to recommend that big league outfielders use smelt nets, too. "They could snare balls that are clearing the fence by ten feet," he said. Heikki said that a catch like that would be a thing of beauty.

I told Heikki that purists probably would not like the idea. He was not too concerned. He didn't like baseball much anyway. "The only time I liked it was when I could come home afterwards with a pail full of smelt," said Heikki, who defied anyone to eat a baseball.

Heikki planned to go to the Monte Carlo the day that Wal-Mart opened. Then he would spend most of the night driving from stream to stream, looking for a run of smelt. If they were running, in the morning he'd come home drunk, soaked, and shaking from the cold. "That's the life," he said happily whenever he thought about such a night.

The Poaching Hall of Fame

Heikki watched Carl Pellonpaa's Sunday morning *Finland Calling* show every week. His all-time favorite show included the interview with the touring Finnish church-league volleyball team from Rovaniemi near the Arctic Circle. He liked the team's guttural one-syllable answers to Carl's questions. "They sound just like my friend Eino," he told me. Heikki wondered why he and his friend had never been on the show. "We're both good men in the woods," said Heikki, who liked to judge people by how well they could handle an ax and a chain saw.

Heikki came over to ask me if I'd call Carl Pellonpaa at TV Six to urge him to have him and Eino on the show. I told him he should call Carl himself, but Heikki was averse to talking to any Finn who wore a suit and spoke grammatically. "I like Carl's show," he said, "but I'll bet he's not worth much out in the jack pine."

I told him that he should stop judging people by the suits they wore. Heikki told me to shut up and get on the phone.

Heikki was averse to talking on the phone himself. If he absolutely had to answer one, he held the receiver firmly in both hands so it couldn't get away. He also held it at arm's length and shouted at it. What Heikki shouted over and over was that Hilda Maki should get off the line. Heikki had a party line with Hilda, and he assumed that she was always listening, but Hilda long since had realized that Heikki never had anything to say. She had ignored his ring for years. Because Heikki had bad hearing, he could not make out what the caller said anyway, so he'd hang up. Then he got out of the room fast before the person called back.

Heikki and Eino wanted to get on *Finland Calling* to talk up an idea they had for setting up a National Poachers' Hall of Fame in Hancock. They even had a site picked out. Since Hancock and Houghton were consolidating their schools, they wanted to use the Hancock High School building, which was right on Route 41. The museum would be similar to the Ski Hall of Fame in Ishpeming. In the display cases, they'd have the actual guns used by famous poachers. "We might have the bones of famous deerhounds, articles of clothing, traps, antlers, stuffed moose and bear, and maybe even a picture or two," said Heikki.

He already knew who he'd have for hall of famers. He and Eino would have to be inducted first. He said he could get letters of recommendation from the guys at the Monte Carlo and maybe even from the DNR, if they cooperated. "Which they never do!" said Heikki. He envisioned a proper inducting process, conducted at the Monte Carlo or at whichever bar the poacher frequented.

Heikki was very interested in the history of poaching. He liked to talk about the good old days of his youth and earlier, when people, like the famous Arvo Heikkinen, could decorate a huge oak in his front yard with the carcasses of thirty-two deer and a bear. Heikki's picture of Arvo's tree, decorated with dead animals for the Christmas season, was one of Heikki's most cherished icons. Where he got the picture, I don't know, but he told me on several occasions about his dancing the polka with Arvo's daughter at a Finnish Temperance Union meeting in the basement of a long-dead church in Redridge.

Another poacher Heikki wanted to honor was Gus Koski. Gus was the guy who shot at the two wardens in 1910 when the wardens threatened to incarcerate Gus' favorite hound. The hound had liked hunting deer with Gus so much that the critter had begun to hunt on his own, and the locals considered that a crime. If anyone was going to eat or otherwise profit from a deer, it had to be Gus, not the hound. "Shooting at the wardens was no big deal," said Heikki. "They were both from Lower Michigan."

"In the good old days, a guy could get away with almost anything," said Heikki. "They used to drive deer to water, using dogs. Then they'd ride up to the deer in a a boat and let 'em have it. Boy, that was the life! Nowadays a guy can't even disturb a little swamp water on his own land without going to jail!"

Heikki had always dreamed of leading the life of a Viking warrior. His favorite character in all literature was Conan the Conqueror in the

Marvel Comics of that title. At the same time, Heikki became disturbed at the downstate hunters who drove north every fall in their expensive four-wheel-drive trucks to get drunk in a hunting camp and occasionally hunt. "If they go near my pile of deer bait, I'll plug 'em," said Heikki.

Heikki finally got it through his thick skull that I was not going to call Carl Pellonpaa at TV Six. "Maybe Eino and I will drive to Marquette and talk to him," said Heikki. He and Eino also wanted to look over the new shipment of drywall at Menard's in the Marquette mall. Both men became really excited by drywall. They could spend hours staring at sheets of the stuff, contemplating constructive possibilities. Heikki was not sure his truck would make it to Marquette. He had 189,000 miles on it, and the tires were thin.

Maybe Carl Pellonpaa would have to wait.

On Guns

Heikki had about six dozen weapons, give or take a half dozen. They sat in various corners of his home, on the racks in his den and in the back window of his pickup. Heikki wasn't a collector in the normal sense, though. He picked up a lot of bargain guns on Saturday nights when drunken friends ran out of money and wanted more booze. Heikki traded the price of a case of Old Milwaukee for a deer rifle or shotgun. Recently, he picked up a couple of assault rifles and a bazooka through just that sort of trade. Heikki fired the bazooka only once. He set a rusty old cast-iron stove out in his back field, stepped back a couple of hundred feet, aimed, and fired. The shell overshot the old stove but blew hell out of the small shed where Hilda Maki kept yard tools. Pieces of Hilda's new power mover sailed all over the neighborhood.

Hilda had been gone at the time, but as soon as she returned, she confronted Heikki, who assured her that the exploding shell had been an act of God. Heikki said that he'd heard a peculiar roar and then a boom. "It's punishment for your lack of neighborliness," he told her.

Heikki thought about hunting with the bazooka. "I could get a whole herd with one shot," he said.

During the day, Heikki kept the bazooka in the bed of his pickup and slept with the thing under the bed. He said it was his hedge against an invasion of the Upper Peninsula by some foreign force—maybe the Russians, Chinese, Canadians, or Downstaters. "There are lots of crazies out there," Heikki said. "I have to be ready to blow them away at any time."

Heikki believed in the survival of the fittest. "Get rid of all laws and all government," he said. "Just like the Old West!" Heikki knew that Finns would survive because they had *sisu* and the Lutheran Church.

Growing Tomatoes

Heikki had an uncommon love of tomatoes fresh from the garden. All winter long, he dreamed of sun-ripened tomatoes. He scorned the tasteless, store-bought variety, which he heaped with verbal abuse.

One year, the weather in the Copper Country was so miserable that few of Heikki's tomato plants survived. Most were killed by a frost in the middle of June. Heikki had plenty of Early Girl plants that were supposed to bear ripe fruit in fifty-two days. He finally got a few small, ripe tomatoes in about a hundred days, just before the fall frost.

Heikki was determined to grow lots of tomatoes, but a repeat of that cool summer's weather was predicted—lots of cold, overcast days with temperatures in the fifties and sixties. He learned all about it from the weather channel, which, he said, was a better predictor than Revelations. Except for the potential effect on his garden, Heikki was delighted at the thought of another summer with fall temperatures because he wouldn't have to take off his long underwear at all. Also, those gray days would be great for fishing.

Heikki hated hot weather and sunshine. He said too much sun brought out the worst in people. They became unbearably spontaneous, friendly, and talkative. He used his Italian friend, Toni, the barber, as an example. Toni always stood close and talked a blue streak while cutting Heikki's hair. Heikki wished that Toni would stand at least a yard from the barber chair and would shut up. "His scissors ought to have long handles like garden shears," he said. Heikki hated to be close to anyone, especially in a public place like a barber shop. He touched his wife once in public in 1952, but that was a mistake. He had thought he was reaching for his hat, and she thought he wanted to hold hands.

In the middle of May, Heikki began tomato plants in pots resting inside all the south-facing windows of his home. He worried about putting them out before warmer weather arrived. After listening to the weather channel, he was afraid to put them out at all.

A few years before, Heikki had kept pigs in a pen behind the barn. He said he liked raising pigs because of the meat and because the smell kept Hilda Maki at a respectable distance. Heikki retrieved the trough from what remained of the pen. After scraping it down, he set it up on sawhorses beneath his wife's new picture window, using it as a giant planter. That way, he reasoned, he would have a few tomatoes no matter how cold it stayed outside.

It remained to be seen if Heikki's long-suffering wife would put up with a trough in her living room, especially when Sunday arrived and her church friends came over for *nisu* and coffee.

Heikki planned to be safely fishing on that day, leaving his defenseless tomato plants to his wife's maternal care. Heikki argued that the way his wife's friends pigged out on sweet rolls and breads and the way they swilled coffee, there ought to be two troughs in the living room. He also predicted that his wife would nurture the plants as if each were a child. She loved *tomaattikalakaaryleet*, he said. That was herring fillets buried in diced tomatoes and dill and baked until flaky.

"Maybe the thought of those tasty fillets will save my plants," he said.

But both of us knew she would get rid of the trough before her church-going friends arrived on Sunday. Heikki would have few tomatoes again.

Taking the Smartass Fishing

Heikki had some of those store-bought Idaho russet potatoes for dinner one night. He was not satisfied. Potatoes were close to Heikki's Finnish heart. He could wax eloquent about potatoes, especially Michigan Reds, Kennebecs, and Green Mountains. New potatoes fresh from the garden sent him into paroxysms of rhapsody. He could also get philosophical about rutabagas, beets, and other root vegetables. Heikki didn't trust any vegetable that grew above the ground (except tomatoes). He said it was the dirt that made vegetables tasty—that they had to be mired. Though it was March, he was anxious to plant his garden with enough potatoes to see him through to the next spring.

Heikki was out surveying the swampy piece of ground he called his garden when his smartass nephew from Lansing arrived for a few days of fishing. "He's got these big thick books that tell him how to catch trout," scoffed Heikki. The nephew tied his own wet and dry flies and had quite a collection.

Heikki took the nephew fishing at his favorite fishing hole, and the nephew immediately hooked a big trout that Heikki had been trying to catch for years. The nephew used a skinny little pole and the lightest of lines. It took him twenty minutes to bring that trout to shore. That really ticked off Heikki, who used a thick pole, thick line, and worms. When he hooked a fish, he hoisted it ashore with the same swiveling of hips and shoulders that he used to heave stove wood onto a truck bed. "That kid's been watching one too many of those fishing shows off Channel Six!" said Heikki, referring to the fact that the nephew then released the trout back into the pool. Heikki said he went nuts watching that fish dance across the pool "like Baryshnikov."

Heikki wouldn't fish with the nephew again. He said he wanted that trout for bragging rights at the Monte Carlo. Plus he wanted to pickle it and use it in his favorite dish—a mixture of cubed cooked beets, raw onions, pickled fish, and mayonnaise.

After his irritating nephew went back to Lansing, Heikki built Hilda Maki some new front steps, using wood he'd soaked in a vat of waterproofing over the winter. Heikki added extra strong railings and dozens of supports. When the steps were done, Heikki told Hilda that she could park a pickup on those steps because "they ain't going nowhere."

Waino Hautamaki, who was well-known for sticking his nose where it didn't belong, reported a murder to the sheriff's department. Driving into his wood lot, he came across a big puddle of blood in one track of the two-track road. Nearby bushes and the lower branches of trees were spattered, and strings of flesh hung from bushes and trees. The sheriff decided that somebody had slaughtered a moose. Apparently, the poacher had dismembered the animal with a chain saw. There had been no arrests, but Heikki suspected the miscreant was the guy who drank at one end of the Monte Carlo bar while his cronies crowded at the other end. Moose muck coated him from the top of his swampers to his baseball cap. Heikki said that he "didn't smell too good either."

Some anonymous person dynamited the pool where Heikki's smartass nephew released the big trout. Heikki said he just happened to hear the explosion and found the trout floating on the surface on its side, its eyes glassy. Heikki said he would show it to the guys at the Monte Carlo, and then he would eat it for supper.

Heikki's Grandson

Heikki was up before dawn, peeing along the edge of what will be his garden when the weather warms up. Then he came over for breakfast and coffee. "Human urine—especially mine—worked like a charm," he told me. "The smell keeps out 'coons, bear, and deer. One whiff, and they scurry right back into the woods. It works pretty well with kids, too." Heikki thought of bottling the stuff and selling it at a roadside stand, along with seedlings and manure.

I told him I'd never heard of such a thing before. He was upset by my ignorance. "Sometimes I feel like I have to dumb down when I'm around you professors," Heikki said.

Heikki's grandson was visiting from Florida. The grandson was the one educated member of Heikki's family. He was named after Heikki, who, in turn, was named after his father. So the grandson called himself Heikki Heikkinen the Third. Heikki thought that was grand.

Heikki was very proud of his grandson and wanted me to get him a job at Suomi College. I asked Heikki what the grandson could do. "Anything," said Heikki, enthusiastically. "President, dean, or whatever."

Heikki and his grandson both were proud alumni of Toivola Elementary. Heikki's formal education stopped there, but the grandson had gone on to get a GED through Adult and Continuing Education night school at Jeffers. Then he made the mistake of signing up for the cosmetology program at Gogebic Community College. "It was a case of mistaken identity," Heikki explained. "My grandson thought cosmetology had something to do with the stars and that he could use it to get a job with NASA."

The grandson transferred to the Jacobetti Center at Northern Michigan University, earned a certificate in welding and completed an

A.A. in Undeclared. Heikki said the grandson then set out to use his natural talents. He got a B.S. in Physical Education from Northern Michigan University, with a specialization in blue-collar sports. "He's certified, accredited, diplomaed, and licensed in fishing, snowmobiling, bowling, outboard boating, the dog paddle, horseshoes, and barroom darts," said Heikki.

"But does he catch fish?" I asked Heikki.

"No, but he knows all sorts of big words that explain why he didn't," said Heikki with awe in his voice. Apparently, the grandson won a scholarship from the Yamaha Snowmobile Corporation while he was at NMU. He also won the Physical Education Department's international prize for a one-paragraph essay on "The Thrill of Bocci Ball."

"I helped him win a couple of other prizes, too," said Heikki. "He and I were both members of the Old Milwaukee Snowmobile Pub Crawl Team of the Keweenaw Peninsula. I also helped him get certified as Magna Cum Laude Road-Sign Shooter by the Colt Firearms Company in 1984."

I told Heikki that his grandson would need more schooling than he had if he wanted a job at Suomi. Heikki said that wouldn't be a problem and pulled a crumpled and stained sheet of paper out of his jacket pocket. It was a copy of the grandson's resumé. Apparently he had an M.A. from a school I never heard of—Paul Bunyan Technological Forestry College in Neck of the Woods, New York. The resumé explained that the grandson had specialized in chain saw management, deforestation, front-end loaders, pulp-truck gearage, and clear cutting. His thesis was titled, "To Hell with Endangered Species," and his special projects paper was on, "Ten Ways to Cheat the Mill—A Practical Guide for U.P. Truckers."

The grandson had an Ed.D. in educational jargon from a little-known state college in California. He had specialized in passive sentences, verbosity, incorrect punctuation, inconclusive conclusions, and the creation of a funereal quality in the classroom. His dissertation was titled, "Bio-energetics and Psychosynthesis in Suburban San Diego Archery Classes—A Transpersonal Profile." That title impressed Heikki no end. "I really like it because I can't even say it!" he said.

The grandson was Associate Dean of Enrolled Deceased Students at Dade County Community College in Miami. He directed a tracking system that allowed deceased victims of drive-by shootings, car jackings, drug overdoses, police brutality, arson, and other assorted pranks to withdraw from classes without penalty. He also directed an educational program for Florida's many death-row inmates. Dade County Community College offered the inmates degrees in gardening, mortuary science, long-range family planning, and winter sports.

I asked Heikki why his grandson wanted a job at Suomi. Heikki didn't know. "What's he like?" I asked.

Heikki explained that the grandson was very much like Heikki himself. "He has no respect for a liberal education and hates liberals of every ilk. He's a lifelong member of the NRA and the Mosquito Inn. He's not an active Lutheran, but he likes their pancake breakfasts and much prefers Lutheran coffee to the Catholic variety," said Heikki.

"How would he do as a leader of our faculty?" I asked.

"He'd respect any professor who chopped his own wood," said Heikki.

I told Heikki that no opening existed at Suomi at the moment. Heikki said I could keep his grandson's resumé just in case something came up in the future. Then he went over to the Monte Carlo to see how his drinking buddies were doing. After he left, I put the resumé in the appropriate place for such a document.

At Toni's Barbershop

Heikki stopped in at Toni's barbershop early one morning. He did not need a haircut; he just wanted Toni to fill him in on the news Heikki couldn't get off the weather channel.

Toni told him about the governor's recent trips to the Copper Country in support of a Republican candidate for office and in support of his own re-election. Heikki wanted to know how the governor got up here, especially since the guy had condemned the former governor for flying all over the state in a plane. Toni explained that the governor had flown. Heikki replied that the governor, being a politician, must be an honest and forthright guy who abhorred hypocrisy. "So what did he fly in?" asked Heikki. "A wheelbarrow?"

Toni was trying to improve himself as a member of Hancock's educated elite. Lately he had been reading the state budget. Toni discovered that Michigan's fastest growing industry was no longer cars. It was prisons. "The state has budgeted twice as much money for prisons as for community colleges," said Toni.

He told Heikki all about the facilities available for the prisoners. "The new prison in Baraga has basketball courts, softball fields, a weight room, free dental and medical care, and good food," explained Toni. He showed Heikki a promotional pamphlet advertising why a guy should commit a crime in order to get in there.

Heikki said he wouldn't mind living in there himself if they'd add a fishing pond and a snowmobile track. Toni showed Heikki a typical weekly menu from the Baraga prison. Heikki looked it over and grunted a couple of times. Except for the fresh asparagus and what Heikki called the "Julius Caesar salad," he figured he could live quite well on state vittles. He'd throw out the foreign stuff though—the tacos and ravioli—and would add more hot dogs, baked beans, and peas. Heikki wondered why America's Most Wanted worked so hard to stay out of today's prisons. "It's like refusing a free membership in a country club. You'd think they'd want it. After all, it beats working," said Heikki.

"But they don't work," said Toni. "They rob banks and fast-food joints and places like that."

Heikki figured that robbing a bank was probably a lot of work. "You have to plan it out, you have to shout and scream and scare folks, and then you have to run like hell with a heavy bag full of money."

Toni had to agree that maybe bank robbery was not all it was cut out to be. Toni pointed out that Heikki would never make it as a bank robber. "How many years has it been since you ran like hell?" Toni asked.

Heikki admitted that it had been maybe thirty-five or forty years. Heikki tried to remember the last time he had run hard but couldn't. He guessed it might have been the time he'd been treed by a moose in Canada.

Toni then mentioned that a mutual friend had recently died in Lake Worth, Florida. He had been eighty-eight. Toni and Heikki agreed that was too young to die. "He'd hardly experienced life," said Heikki.

Toni had further educated himself recently by checking out the costs of funeral homes. "They take a bundle," he said.

Heikki agreed. Heikki said that when his time came, he wanted to be incinerated. "Afterwards you can take my ashes to the town dump and scatter them with the rest of the garbage," said Heikki, who had his own weird interpretation of Lutheran theology and the Resurrection. "When they resurrect old refrigerators and bedsprings, they can bring me back, too," he said.

The New Barbeque Grill

Heikki's nephew gave him a new barbeque grill for his eighty-seventh birthday. Heikki had destroyed his first grill after it ruined a perfectly good parts-missing turkey from Jim's Foodmart in Houghton. Ever since, Heikki had been perfectly happy baking his potatoes, frying his steak, and eating his canned peas floating in water. Heikki cursed the nephew considerably when he saw the new grill, but under unrelenting pressure from the rest of the family, Heikki finally agreed to give the infernal machine one more chance to ruin a perfectly good meal.

This time, Heikki deferred to common sense and decided to grill bratwurst. Brats were cheaper than turkey and less bothersome—or so Heikki thought. His granddaughter, who worked as a secretary in the front office of the Green Bay Packers, had become a fanatical Packer backer and a kind of Wisconsinite by default, despite her Copper Country roots. She sent Heikki a couple of free Packer tickets every year, but Heikki so far had declined to go. He wanted the granddaughter to guarantee ahead of time that Brett Favre would sprain an ankle, break an arm, or otherwise maim himself in a fashion appropriate to the frustration he had caused Heikki's bar-hopping geriatric friends in recent years.

So far, the granddaughter only guaranteed that the tickets were on the fifty-yard line. Heikki felt guilty that the girl wasted so many tickets on him. He knew she would have liked to use them herself. So, when she told him that she had a special Wisconsin recipe for grilled bratwurst, Heikki listened and then followed her directions. He bought some fresh brats instead of his usual precooked Vollwerth's. He simmered the brats for a few minutes in a mixture of beer and onions. Then he grilled the brats to a golden brown and ate them on a bun, with his usual mustard, catsup, minced onion, and pickle.

I asked him how they were.

Heikki said the brats were passable, but the simmered beer was awful.

I told him he wasn't supposed to drink the beer—that it was a kind of marinade.

Heikki said he thought that was the case, but he hadn't been sure, so he drank all of it. Plus, he hated the idea of not drinking the contents of an open can of Old Milwaukee.

I asked him to explain exactly how the beer tasted.

Heikki said the onion made it a bit chewy, and the grease certainly oiled his insides. "Plus it was very warm—like year-old coffee," he said. "And the boiling made it flat."

Heikki said he was definitely done with grills and all other new-fangled ways of cooking. He couldn't see spending time and effort on a contraption that made food taste like the inside of a furnace and ruined the contents of a perfectly good can of beer.

Last year Heikki's birthday was ruined, too. The day turned out to be perfect—with a clear blue sky, bright sunshine, and warm temperatures. Weather like that meant that fish didn't bite. Heikki spent most of the day out on Portage Lake in his little boat and never caught a thing. He had been hoping for overcast skies and maybe a cold, light rain. The good weather forced him to contemplate the meaning of life. Heikki tended to get existential angst when the sun shone. His Finnish blood preferred the kind of gray weather that brooded. Broody weather made his blood sing and the fish bite.

Let's hope that this year on his birthday the weather is appropriately lousy.

Season for Colds

Any season is a season for colds in the Copper Country. On one occasion, Heikki took his boat out on Portage Lake to do a little fishing. As usual, he slipped quickly into a catatonic state after his first cast. It was cold and rainy all day. By the time Heikki redocked hours later, his sinuses were plugged solid. The infection soon spread into his ear.

Heikki took a sauna and went to bed, but he couldn't sleep. His aching ear kept him up until three a.m. Then he drove himself to the emergency room. The doctor on duty assured Heikki that he had a cold in his sinuses and ear. Heikki said he already knew that.

The doctor tried to give Heikki a couple of those twenty-dollar hospital aspirins, but Heikki said he didn't want them. Instead he offered to sell the hospital a big bottle of Norwich brand aspirins he had picked up at K-Mart for a couple of bucks. Heikki said he'd sell them for only ten dollars apiece, and the hospital could still turn a tidy profit. The doctor ignored his offer. He charged Heikki only ten dollars for not taking the proffered aspirin. He also put a forty-dollar drop in Heikki's ear and wrote up a sixty-dollar prescription. Then he tossed in another forty dollars for telling Heikki he had a cold. The doctor wanted to keep Heikki overnight for observation, but the bed would have cost Heikki's pension for the next three months.

Heikki said that going to the emergency room was the smartest thing he had ever done. He said the bill acted as a kind of magic elixir. His whole body knew instantly that it couldn't afford to be sick. It quickly evolved into a new life form resistant to cold germs. By the next afternoon, Heikki's sinuses had drained, the infection had fled his ear, and he was back on the lake in his boat.

Heikki's Last Revenge

A week ago last Tuesday, Heikki sat down to a breakfast of pickled pig's feet, King Oscar sardines, limburger cheese, and saltines. Afterwards, he washed the stuff down with a half dozen cups of steaming black coffee. He told his wife he felt tired, lay down on the couch and died. He was just a few days short of his eighty-eighth birthday.

His buddies at the Monte Carlo blamed his death on the limburger. "The stuff takes a strong constitution. Limburger is for young, sober men. Women should never touch it," said Waino Hautamaki.

"It's for young men with hair on their chest," agreed Uno Wainio.

Heikki's buddies were surprised to hear that Heikki had left a will. In it he had asked to be cremated, with his ashes to be scattered at the town dump. The cremation took place at a local funeral home a week ago last Thursday. Afterwards, Heikki's long-suffering widow debated what to do about the ashes. She knew she could not fulfill his wishes concerning the dump. The idea of scattering his ashes there revolted her. She suspected Heikki had suggested it just to embarrass her.

The ashes had been placed in a shiny copper urn by the funeral home. At first, the widow thought she would put the urn in the sauna since Heikki had loved taking saunas so much. But she didn't want to sit naked in front of her dead husband's ashes. "Maybe he'll be leering at me from inside the urn," she said to her neighbor, Hilda Maki. Then she remembered that other women occasionally came over for a sauna. "I can't have young, naked women frolicking in front of my husband," she told Hilda.

"Heikki won't know the difference. He's gone," said Hilda, who felt only elation that her long-time nemesis was dead.

Next, Heikki's widow thought she'd put the urn on the coffee table

74

in the living room.

"With all those doilies that he always hated?" asked Hilda.

In the end, the widow put the urn in the back of the top shelf of the refrigerator, where Heikki had always kept his Old Milwaukee.

Down at the Monte Carlo, the proprietor heard about Heikki's demise and figured his year's profits would be down considerably. He'd read somewhere that a cafe in Paris had a table permanently reserved for Ernest Hemingway. So, the proprietor cut a cardboard flap off the bottom of an Old Milwaukee case and used a black magic marker to write RESERVED HEIKKI HIEKKINEN on it. He bent the cardboard in the middle for support and set the sign on a table in the back of the bar. Later in the day, as Heikki's geriatric buddies gathered to down a few in Heikki's honor, they noticed the sign and thought it was a nice touch.

Eino Aho said they ought to let Heikki have one last night on the town. Eino drove out to Heikki's place and asked the widow for the ashes. "I'm thinking of scattering them in Lake Superior," she said but agreed that Eino and the other guys could have the ashes for a few hours. "Bring them back in the morning," she said. She assumed they'd treat Heikki's ashes with the same respect that they'd treated Heikki in life.

Eino returned to the Monte Carlo with the ashes just as the place was invaded by a large and rowdy crowd of college students from Michigan Tech. The students bought the regulars several rounds, and soon everyone in the bar glowed. Heikki's ashes were passed around with reverence. Several guys bought rounds for Heikki and then drank them themselves.

A half-hour after the departure of the college crowd, Eino noticed that the RESERVED HEIKKI HEIKKINEN sign was missing. "One of those damned kids from the college swiped it," Uno Wainio said. "He's probably having a laugh right now with his friends at Tech."

"It's no big loss," said the proprietor. "I'm certainly not going to call the cops because some college kid stole a cardboard sign off a table. I can make another. Besides, I need the table. It was just a thought—like a Hallmark card."

After that, everybody began to do some determined drinking. Heikki's ashes continued to make the rounds. Around eleven, many of the regulars left for the Mosquito Inn. Heikki's ashes went along in the back of Arvid Ahonen's pickup. After the Mosquito, the boys visited the Pub, the Cozy Corner, and the Range Lounge in quick succession. Somewhere in these, Heikki's ashes spent a few minutes in the possession of Veikko Liimatainen. After that, Heikki's old buddies had drinks at the Green Lantern, the B and B, the Ambassador, and the Uphill. They played pool at Partanen's, ate pizzas and pickled fish at Quincy's, had more drinks and participated in a darts tournament at the Loading Zone, and finally settled down for some serious drinking at the Keg.

By then, no one had even the vaguest idea what had happened to Heikki's ashes. "That son of a bitch always was hard to keep track of," said a very drunk Finn when the loss was discovered.

"It's because he drank in so many places," said someone else.

The next afternoon, Eino drove over to the widow's place to tell her that he'd lost Heikki's ashes. The widow was not as upset as he had expected her to be. "I didn't know what to do with that urn anyway," she said. "It doesn't fit with my decor."

"Maybe he'll still be found," said Eino. "The boys and I are still looking. Maybe if someone else finds the urn, they'll throw it away, and it'll end up in the dump anyway. That's where Heikki wanted to be."

A couple of days later, one of the guys found the urn, with the ashes still inside, mixed with some pop cans and rusty razor blades under the back seat of his old Chevy. He had no idea how the urn had gotten there and couldn't remember having driven the Chevy that night, but he knew that he had to return it. But first he went into the Monte Carlo for a few drinks. The few soon stretched into many. By the time the old guy left the bar, he had great difficulty locating his car and then even more difficulty getting in. After he had found the ignition and the steering wheel, he headed for Heikki's place. He hadn't told anyone about the recovery of the miscreant ashes because he didn't want to be ribbed by the other guys.

It was a moonless night, and the road kept leaping out of view—sometimes to the left, and sometimes to the right, and at least once straight overhead. The old guy reached what he thought was Heikki's place about three a.m.

He fell out of his car with the urn held tightly in both hands. He staggered to his feet, heard a dog bark somewhere and was sure the beast was going to lunge out of the dark and take off his leg. For a moment, he wasn't sure what to do, but then he remembered that, fifty years earlier, he had been a pretty respectable pitcher for a team from Tapiola. He took the urn in his right hand, wound up, and heaved it at Heikki's widow's front door. Unfortunately, in his drunken stupor, he'd parked by Hilda Maki's place by mistake. The urn arched out toward the house and crashed explosively through Hilda's new French windows.

Hilda heard the sound of a departing car moments after the shattering glass woke her. She hurried downstairs, flipped on the light, and found the urn on the living room floor, surrounded by glass shards. The ashes had streamed several yards across the carpet. "Damn that Heikki!" Hilda said to herself. "Even after he's dead, he keeps driving me crazy!"

Hilda spent the better part of an hour picking up glass, surveying damage, and covering the hole in the window with cardboard to keep out the cold. Then she got out the vacuum, plugged it in, put it on full power, and proceeded to vacuum up the ashes. "Now I've finally got you!" she said as the last of Heikki was sucked up the tube. Unfortunately, some glass shards were sucked up, too. The shards cut through the bag inside the machine. Then the shards and the remains of Heikki blew out through the bottom of the bag and into the vacuum's motor. The motor made a peculiar rasping sound and then died suddenly.

Hilda opened the machine and discerned the damage. Her new Electrolux seemed to be ruined beyond repair. Worse, when she tipped it up in order to see better, the glass and ashes fell out onto the rug again. "Damn you, Heikki!" she cried. "I hate you, Heikki! You drive me crazy!"

The ashes didn't say anything.

Hilda noticed.

"At last I get the last word!" she said.

Then she went back to bed.

❖   ❖   ❖   ❖   ❖

Finnish women have a strong sense of privacy, which they violate only on Sunday morning after church when they gather to gossip over *nisu* and coffee. Then everything comes out. Hence, every Finn in the Copper

Country soon knew Hilda's story.

Finnish men have even a stronger sense of privacy than do the women. But when they get drunk, everything comes out—often in a maudlin and oddly pitched voice. Hence, every Finn in the Copper Country soon knew all about the misadventures of Heikki's ashes.

Since then, the legend of Heikki has grown. Patrons inside the Monte Carlo have seen Heikki sitting in his pickup in the shadows outside the bar. A couple of guys swore they saw him on the snowmobile trail leading to the Mosquito. Others said they saw him fishing on Portage Lake. Somebody's cousin wrote to say that he saw Heikki shouldering an ax in the post office in Ashtabula, Ohio.

Petri Pekkala, one of Heikki's many former snowmobile buddies, said that Heikki was in hot competition with Elvis for the greatest number of North American post-dead sightings of a single individual.

Wherever he is, I hope that Heikki is enjoying his posthumous fame.

An Odd Collection of Finns

Sulo

Sulo was born into a large, destitute family in Finland during World War II. The family's fortunes did not improve with the end of the war.

One morning when Sulo was five, his mother sewed a tag to his jacket. The tag contained the address of a woman in Hancock, Michigan. The woman was a friend of Sulo's parents who had emigrated years earlier to the United States. The tag was sewn with care to make sure that Sulo arrived at her house. Then his parents took Sulo to the airport in Helsinki and put him on a plane for America.

Today Sulo has four memories of Finland. He remembers traveling by boat to Helsinki from the island where his family lived. He remembers being hanged by older boys when he was about three and being rescued by his mother. He has two particularly vivid memories that, even today, can cause him to break out into a sweat. He remembers falling off a dock and nearly drowning before being rescued by his mother and sitting on that plane at the airport in Helsinki, peering out the little round window at his parents. He knew he would never see them again.

He never did.

"All the time I was on that plane, I was waiting for my mother to rescue me," he told me.

But she never did.

As a consequence of these last two memories, Sulo was terrified of airplanes and boats. He hadn't been in either since 1946. He won't even cross a bridge because, for him, it's like taking off in a plane. To get to Lower Michigan he drives straight south to Chicago, then circles around the bottom of Lake Michigan and drives north again. When crossing the lift bridge between Hancock and Houghton, he closes his eyes.

In Hancock Sulo refused to speak for a long time, though his new mother could speak Finnish and tried to get him to open up to her. Eventually he spoke—in English. He hasn't spoken Finnish since. He bet he was the only person on Earth who forgot his own language.

He may be right.

In Hancock, Sulo took the last name of his new mother. He attended her church, ate her food, slept in one of the beds in her house. But a little piece of him always remained the outsider. That was the piece from Finland. He never let the new mother have that part of himself because deep down inside, he knew that was the essential part.

It made him who he was.

Once some guests who only spoke Finnish visited Sulo's American mother. His American mother asked Sulo to greet them in Finnish. He refused. His American mother slapped his face very hard. Several times. She cried out of frustration.

Sulo did not cry.

Each Christmas, Sulo's real mother called from Finland to say hello. She did that for forty years. Sulo felt more and more distant from that strange, foreign voice with each passing year. "Who is this woman?" he said to himself.

Sulo graduated from Hancock High School and went off to college at Northern Michigan University in Marquette. He studied Business Administration, a field of study he hated but one his new mother and his new mother's friends and apparently everybody else in Hancock saw as practical and worthwhile. The Vietnam War was in full swing. Sulo hated the war. He grew long hair and a beard and openly proclaimed his pacifism. That irritated the relatives and friends of his American mother. Sulo had been born during the first Winter War with the Russians. He and his family had suffered terribly through that war, through World War II and through the second war with the Russians. The way that Sulo understood it, he had hated war right from birth. So when he thought he might be drafted, he briefly went to Canada. He took along an ax to make a living and an extra shirt and underwear.

After Sulo returned, his American mother died very slowly of cancer. Sulo nursed her for months, right through to the bitter end. He attended the funeral and said good-bye at the grave site. Then he took back his name from Finland and left the Upper Peninsula.

Under his birth name, he enrolled in college in Chicago and later in Missoula, Montana. He studied subjects he loved—music and theology. Eventually he became a minister and musician. He grew long hair and a beard and played the kantele. He reminded listeners of Vainamoinen and of other wizards of the mythic old. He returned to the Upper Peninsula to play guitar in a polka band. He wrote songs about U.P. Finns who, try as hard as they might, never returned to Finland.

A few years ago, one of Sulo's sisters called from Finland and said she was coming for a visit. She and he rediscovered each other's worlds. She showed him pictures of Finland and of his Finnish family. He fed her corn on the cob, baked potatoes, and American steaks. They got along wonderfully.

Then one of Sulo's brothers came for a visit. The brother tried to get Sulo to visit him in Finland. Something always interfered—like Sulo's fear of airplanes and boats.

But maybe soon he'll make the trip. It won't help him to rediscover his mother. She has reached that age where she now lives permanently in the distant past. She is also bedridden. Sometimes from her bed she tells her visiting children that little Sulo is playing down the street. "Go and call Sulo for supper," she says to her grown children, some of whom can't even remember Sulo.

Sulo thought he might be able to visit Finland by walking over the top of the world in midwinter when the Arctic Ocean was frozen. "It can't be far in a straight line from the top of Canada to the top of Finland," he said. Another way might be to drug himself so heavily that he wouldn't know he was on a plane.

His brother persists in wanting Sulo in Finland. I wish him luck.

Little Reino

Little Reino St. Pierre had been confused all of his life, and, with a half-Finnish Lutheran and half-French Catholic name like that, it was understandable.

Reino was raised as an only child in an ultra-strict Lutheran home. His mother allowed him to read only four books when he was growing up: the Bible, a biography of Martin Luther for children, the *Lutheran Guide to Healthy Living*, and *The Power of Positive Thinking* by Norman Vincent Peale. Little Reino decided to pass on all four and grow up pretty much knowing nothing about everything.

Most of Reino's problems had to do with his mother, Esther. Esther came from an extended Apostolic Lutheran family of approximately 350 brothers, sisters, nieces, nephews, aunts, uncles, great aunts, great uncles, grandparents, and cousins. Esther was the oldest daughter of a church-centered couple that eventually reared twenty-two children of their own. Just the responsibility of trying to remember the names of all those relatives and helping to raise all those brothers and sisters quickly pushed Esther over the edge. Suspecting that her parents' fecundity would never end and that she would be changing her siblings' diapers for the rest of her life, Esther eloped at sixteen in 1947 with a French-Canadian woodcutter named François. The elopement served its purpose because her parents didn't want much to do with her anymore.

But poor Esther was never able to unravel the conflicts between her Apostolic Lutheran upbringing and her husband's Catholicism. Her conservative Catholic in-laws seemed to take the cue from her parents and wouldn't have much to do with her either, although they still treated their son as if he were God's gift to the world. Esther felt that she had been excommunicated from her own church, and she found the Catholic service hideously pagan. Eventually, she found safety in a Missouri Synod Lutheran Church pastored by a thin, small man with a high voice named Alvar Ahonen.

Alvar was one of those modern preachers with a sociology degree. He had learned to shake his head at everybody in a very concerned and benevolent way. Unfortunately, he spent more time at Sunday morning services looking at his own feet than projecting his squeaky voice. For Esther, who needed respite from the emotional mess of her life, the pastor was a godsend—a safe and mediocre bore.

Little Reino passionately hated those Sunday morning services. He'd rather have been out with his dad cutting wood and communing with nature. Reino hated the remainder of Sunday, too. While his dad visited with *his* parents and invariably ate dinner with them, Reino remained at home as Esther prepared tea and bakery for her church friends. Then Reino had to sit quietly through the afternoon in the darkened living room while Esther and her lady friends chatted about the church and stuffed themselves on *nisu* and cookies.

Every arm and back of every chair in that room was anointed with a doily. Reino hated the doilies. They became the focus of all his pent-up anger concerning those boring Sunday afternoons. Reino eventually formed an uncontrollable phobia about doilies. In his adulthood, if he noticed a doily on a chair he would run screaming out of the room, the hair on the back of his neck standing straight up.

When Reino was in the fifth grade, he committed his first major sin. While his mother was getting a prescription for her nerves filled at the drugstore, he stole the Classic Comics version of *Moby Dick* from the comics rack. That night, he read it straight through.

Captain Ahab fascinated him. Reino loved the man for his madness—for the way he had set out to destroy the white whale, the most magnificent creature in God's creation. All his life Reino had wanted to do something like that—to create a magnificent mess out of the stifling orderliness of his and his mother's lives. His mother had always been fanatic about cleanliness and order. She had always required that dirty dishes be rinsed immediately after use and put in the sink to be washed as soon as a few had collected, that clothes always be hung where they belonged or placed in the proper drawer, that anything spilled be wiped up immediately. "If Ahab had known my mother," Reino told himself, "he would have set fire to her house."

In seventh grade, Reino got a paper route and used his earnings to buy a Greek fisherman's hat from the Army Surplus store in Houghton. The hat was the closest in appearance to Ahab's sea captain's cap that he could find.

In eighth grade, Reino saved enough money to buy a peacoat to go with the hat. By then, the other kids in town thought that Reino was very weird. They nearly always left him out of their organized activities. Reino would curse them from the sidelines, using the same kind of apocalyptical language his mother often used to discipline him. "His wrath will strike you down!" he'd shout, or, "The Lord is ever watching!"

"Tell Him to watch this!" Joe Maki shouted back one time and promptly smacked a home run over the left field fence in a pickup game on the Little League diamond in Hancock.

When Reino graduated from high school at the bottom of his class in 1965, the sixties were in full swing. America was becoming disorderly and more than a little bit crazy. Nuts like Reino were all over the place. Reino loved it. That summer, he helped his dad load pulp logs onto their truck and transport them to the mill in Ontonagon. His dad paid him a regular salary. He bought himself an old black Hudson Hornet and wrote *Pequod* on the doors, hood, roof, and trunk in pink paint. The car didn't look much like Ahab's ship, but it would have to do.

In the evening, Reino would put on his peacoat and Greek fisherman's hat and imagine that he looked just like Gregory Peck, who had played Ahab in John Huston's 1956 film version of *Moby Dick*. He would drive around in his old car, pretending the car was a ship. He spent hours looking long and hard for something magnificent and Godly to harpoon with his front bumper.

Late one evening, when he was cruising a side road off Quincy Hill, he spotted a young man walking on the side of the road near Hilda Maki's place. The guy had long hair, a long beard, a flowing white daishiki, sandals, and jeans. Reino knew the man had to be Jesus because he looked just like the pictures of Jesus on the wall in his mother's house, except for the blue jeans. Reino decided to destroy him with his car, just as Ahab had tried to destroy the whale with his ship.

Reino speeded up and veered the *Pequod* right at the young man, but the guy was a lot nimbler than he looked. He leaped aside and gave

Reino the finger as his Hudson roared by.

Reino's car fishtailed, and then careened off the road, down the bank, across a corner of Hilda Maki's yard, and straight into her hen-house. The car came to a stop more or less intact but with the grill entangled in chicken wire and the windshield coated with feathers, shattered eggs, and chicken feces.

After that, Reino put away forever his Hudson and his dreams of Melvillean grandeur and became a spiritless and insipid man. In 1975, he finally completed an A.A. degree in General Studies at Suomi College. Today he sells term life insurance to those crazy enough to trust him with their family's future. He is a regular in several Hancock bars but usually sits alone in the back of the Monte Carlo with a glass of Old Milwaukee in front of him. He still wears his peacoat and Greek fisherman's hat, but the fire has gone out of his eyes. He lives alone with his mother in the same house on Ingot Street in which he grew up. He avoids the house's living room and its many doilies. His father died years ago in a boating accident on Lake Superior.

Before his death, Heikki, also a regular at the Monte Carlo, of course, gave Reino an illustrated copy of the *Kalevala*. Lord knows what effect that'll have on the guy.

Jussi Aho

Jussi Aho was a recluse who had lived alone in a two-room shack in Misery Bay for as long as anybody could remember. He owned a couple of half-starved huskies that somebody had given him, but the dogs didn't offer much companionship. Jussi kept them outside on long leashes attached to a wire that ran from the corner of the shack to a maple. The ground where the dogs ran was bare earth from their claws. The area was littered with butcher scraps gnawed to the quick and with dog feces.

The dogs had grown wild from lack of domestication and invariably lunged at the rare visitor to Jussi's shack, threatening to rip off a leg or tear open a throat. Wise visitors approached the shack in a wide loop so that the frustrated dogs were left to roar in anger and lunge until the leashes snapped them back to earth.

Jussi said he needed the dogs for protection. "They keep away bears and burglars," he said, but, of course, he had nothing a burglar would want, and bears are not overly fond of Van Camp's beans in tomato sauce, which was pretty much all Jussi ate.

Jussi was badly deformed—a bent and lopsided dwarf whose badly fractured English was spiced with broken Finnish. Jussi had lived all but the first five years of his life in Misery Bay. The oldest child of Finnish immigrants, he had been born with his deformity, with the left side of his body twisted grotesquely. When his parents left Finland for Michigan, Jussi had just begun school. In Michigan, Jussi's education was sporadic at best. For several years, his parents never sent him at all. Then they sent him when he wasn't needed at home, but that was rare. Jussi was a very dependable child who did what he was told and who always completed a task. His parents presented him with a new sibling every one of . their first eight years in America, and Jussi helped his mother with the children and chores.

Eventually, Jussi's brothers and sisters went to school, graduated, found work, married, and settled down in the Keweenaw to raise families. Jussi remained at home, and as his parents grew old, he took care of them. His miner father died of lung hemorrhage at sixty-two, and his mother died of thrombosis within the year. Jussi tried to live in the family home alone, but the memories were too painful. He tore the place down and used some of the lumber to build his rude shack.

Jussi's lonely life did not stop him from dreaming grandly. He received a disability check from the state, and he never worked except at odd jobs given to him by pitying neighbors, so he had lots of time to dream. On Saturdays, Jussi often walked to the Mosquito Inn, where he would voice those dreams while munching down bag after bag of potato chips and talking to patrons more than he'd drink. It was as if the silence of his lonely week required that he talk all day.

Jussi loved to tell local customers how he had fought in the war from the beaches of Normandy to the Rhine. Other days he told how he had fought from Sicily to the Brenner Pass in Austria. Everyone knew he was lying, but that didn't bother them or him. Jussi was a character, and characters were supposed to lie. They'd buy him drinks and chips, and, when his banter got to be too much, they'd pass him on to someone else. "Why don't you go and tell Eino that one," one would say, and so Jussi would make the rounds.

If the Mosquito's customers included hunters or snowmobilers from downstate, Jussi would tell them elaborate tales about his days as a top chef in the best restaurants of Chicago and New York and how he had studied pastry making in Vienna. He wrote what he said were recipes in an illegible hand on napkins and passed these around. Locals called these Jussi's hen scratchings. They made him the butt of jokes. "How did you reach the stuff in the cupboards?" they'd tease him. "Did they supply you with a ladder in those fancy restaurants?"

Jussi dreamed all his life of visiting Finland, the land of his parents. One day, he shocked everyone at the Mosquito by announcing that he'd saved enough for a ticket. "I'm going to Finland this week," he said. They assumed this was another of his fabrications, but he produced a bus ticket to Duluth and a FinnAir ticket to Helsinki. One of his brothers in

Houghton had gotten him the tickets and had arranged everything.

It was a one-way ticket. "I'm never coming back to this old junk place," Jussi said, pronouncing the "j" in "junk" like a "y."

A few days later, he was gone. The huskies remained on their leashes for a couple of days, wild with hunger. Then some humane soul shot and buried them.

Weeks after Jussi's departure, some neighbors visited his shack. They broke the lock and, out of curiosity, surveyed his meager belongings. He'd never had much—a bedspring in one corner covered with a lumpy mattress, a couple of broken-backed chairs, a shelf of canned beans and Vienna sausages, and a pot-bellied wood stove. A few tools lay scattered around with a few kitchen pots and pans and dishes. A water bucket sat beneath a rude sink.

The town pretty much forgot about Jussi. A few years later, a Painesdale relative flew to Finland to visit relatives and to tour the old country. The relatives helped the Painesdale man locate Jussi.

After his return to America, the Painesdale relative spent a Saturday at the Mosquito and told everybody what had happened to Jussi. "He got off the plane in Helsinki, and the Finns thought he was crazy," explained the relative. "Maybe it was because he wore his red-and-black plaid wool cap with earflaps, his heavy yellow-and-black plaid flannel shirt, his green wool pants, suspenders, and swampers."

"What was the matter with that?" asked another Misery Bay man, who was wearing that same garb.

"It was a hot July day, and Helsinki is a sophisticated city," said the relative. The relative explained that no one in Finland could understand either Jussi's English or his Finnish. They locked him up in a hospital, where the relative had spent an afternoon with him. Jussi had said that the food was very good and that he had a sauna.

"The hospital is new and clean," said the relative. " Jussi is very happy. He told me it is better in the nut house in Finland than it ever was in Misery Bay.

The story circulated through the Mosquito. Everyone found it wonderfully funny. "Jussi's found paradise in a Finnish asylum," they said. "He has free food, clean sheets, and a sauna. He can probably watch TV. What more can a man hope for?"

Uncle Jussi

My Uncle Jussi worked hard all week in the copper mines of northern Michigan and drank very hard all weekend at home.

Uncle Jussi was one of those shy and humble Finns who spent a lot of time shifting weight, grinning foolishly, and saying nothing. My father's sister, Aunt Sarah, was equally shy. They only came to visit when there was no other recourse—Uncle Jussi needed to borrow something right away, or Aunt Sarah needed to see her brother on some other family business. Usually Uncle Jussi stood outside our door, fiddling with the wool cap he wore winter and summer and speaking rapidly to my father in a hushed Finnish. Before they drove away, my father would walk with Jussi out to his rusting green Chevrolet pickup and say a few words to Aunt Sarah, who sat hunched in the passenger seat, her hair hidden by a scarf that tightly encircled her face.

They had two sons, Waino and Toivo. Waino was the older. He was also the normal one. He played with other kids when he was growing up, starred at basketball in high school, graduated with honors, married his French-Canadian sweetheart, and moved to Connecticut, where he worked in a supermarket.

Toivo was even shyer than his parents. He never played with other kids as a child, rarely spoke during his high school years, and continued to live at home after graduation. He cut wood on the family lot and helped his mother with the animals—a cow, a few laying hens, a nanny goat, and a half-wild husky they kept leashed by the front door.

Years passed. Uncle Jussi and Aunt Sarah grew old. Toivo began to lose his hair but not his shyness. The family still lived with an outhouse, a pump at the sink instead of faucets, and no phone or television. They had a small radio in the kitchen.

One day, while Jussi was at work, Sarah suffered a stroke and collapsed onto the kitchen floor with a loud thump. Toivo dragged her limp body into the living room, where the carpet was softer than the kitchen linoleum. He wrapped his mother in the afghan from the couch and then stood in mute terror, wondering what to do. He was too shy to run to the neighbors' and ask for help, and Jussi had the Chevrolet. Finally, Toivo decided to walk the three miles to town and call his brother, Waino, in Connecticut. He figured Waino would know what to do. He found his brother's phone number in the kitchen on his mother's note pad. With it in hand, he set out. Their nearest neighbor was out in the field working. He waved, and Toivo summoned up enough courage to wave back, but he didn't say anything. A mile from town, a man he knew slowed his truck to give Toivo a lift, but Toivo was too shy to get in. He waved the man off.

Finally, Toivo reached the public phone booth. Thank God there was no one around, or he might not have had the courage to try to make his first ever phone call. Thank God he also had a quarter in his pocket. Toivo read the directions printed on the phone three times before he dared put the quarter into the slot and dial. When the operator's voice came on the line, he nearly died of fright. She almost cut him off before he finally managed to tell her that it was a collect call.

Toivo told Waino what had happened. Waino told him to call the local hospital in Hancock. "Their number is in the phone book," said Waino. Toivo panicked and hung up.

From Connecticut, Waino called the hospital in Michigan, and an ambulance was immediately dispatched to pick up Sarah. Toivo saw it pass with its lights flashing as he walked home. Then he saw it again, heading for the hospital. He thought of waving it down but didn't want to trouble them. His mother was already in a hospital bed by the time Toivo returned home and sat down to a supper of canned beans and Spam.

By some miracle, Sarah survived. She walked with a noticeable limp and couldn't do fine work with her fingers, but otherwise she seemed okay.

A few months later, Jussi had a stroke, too. He had driven into town on a Saturday morning to mail a sweepstakes form back to *Reader's Digest* so he could collect his ten million dollars. He came out of the post office, climbed into his truck, and discovered that he couldn't move the entire left side of his body. He sat all day in his Chevrolet in front of the post office, paralyzed with fear and shame and desperately wanting a cup of coffee. People he knew passed and waved. Jussi waved back with his right hand.

Toward dark, Jussi could move his left side a little. With great difficulty, he got the truck started and drove home. He managed to park in the driveway but couldn't get out. The barking husky alerted Toivo, who came to the rescue. Toivo carried his father into the house and laid him on the couch. He recognized the symptoms. While Sarah tried to get a little coffee down Jussi's throat, Toivo hunted around for a quarter, grabbed his brother's phone number off the kitchen note pad and drove the Chevrolet to the public phone in town. Again he called Waino collect. Again Waino called the local hospital from Connecticut. Again the ambulance dashed to the rescue, arriving at the house about the same time Toivo did.

The ambulance crew rolled Jussi from the couch onto a stretcher and carried him to the ambulance. On the way to the hospital, one of them asked Jussi what had happened. Jussi slurred his words but told them. "While you sat there all day," one of the crew asked, "why didn't you ask for help from somebody walking by?"

"Then who would drive my truck home?" Jussi asked.

Within months, Jussi recovered. Now he's retired and has stopped drinking. He and Sarah limp about the house, waited on by the silent Toivo who saved their lives.

They are all still shy and humble. Some Finns are just that way.

Turfy Turpeinen

Turfy Turpeinen was a born loser. As a little kid, he was the sort who could trip and fall down while standing stationary on a perfectly flat surface. When he was a little older, he managed somehow to skin his knee and bloody his nose while competing in a neighborhood marbles match. In high school, he had no friends. Desperate for acceptance by his peers, he joined the ski team. Initially, the coach assigned him to the downhill race team because Turfy could go very fast in a straight line. Unfortunately, the ski hill was not absolutely straight, and Turfy remembered halfway down that he had no idea how to turn or stop. He did eventually stop, of course. Billy Ranta, who was the best skier on the team, said it was the first time he'd ever seen someone wearing skis catapulting through saplings.

Because Turfy was a Finn, the coach assumed that Turfy had *sisu*, which he defined as a kind of foolhardy courage disattached from the thinking part of the brain. All of the guys with *sisu* were assigned to the jumping team. The coach was Cornish, so what did he know? The high school jumping platform and chute had been sawed and hammered together out of old barn wood by the father of one of the competitors. It was a bit rickety but served its purpose. A ladder ran up the back side of the platform. The platform itself rose only about twenty feet in the air, and the chute gave enough speed for about a ninety-foot jump.

Turfy made his first climb up the ladder just after going into the saplings. He still felt a little dizzy but managed to place his skis in the grooves on top. He snapped his boots into the bindings and was ready. To get a fast start, he grasped each side of the launching platform and leaned back in a crouch. But his hands slipped, he slid backwards and plummeted headfirst off the back of the platform. The tips of his skis struck every rung of the ladder on the way down. The sound of the skis whacking the rungs reminded Billy Ranta of someone playing chopsticks on the piano.

Turfy struck a deep drift head first and was buried with only his lower legs and his skis showing. After the other jumpers dug Turfy out, Billy cursed him. "Dammit, Turfy, you broke two rungs right off the platform and splintered the others," he said. "Next time you fall off the back, be more careful!"

After that, Turfy tried baseball. On the first day of practice, the coach sent Turfy out to right field to shag flies. Then the coach lofted a soft fly ball out to right but nowhere near Turfy. Instead, the ball sailed down the right field line. Turfy ran at full speed after the fly ball, but it was dropping rapidly as he approached. Turfy threw himself into the air, his whole body parallel to the ground. He stretched his gloved arm out toward the ball, straining to reach it. Unfortunately, Turfy had considerably misjudged the direction of the ball's descent. The ball struck Turfy in the face, breaking his nose.

After that, Turfy gave up on sports and became very quiet. He sat in the back of the room in each of his classes and only spoke if spoken to. He was too shy even to glance at the girls. In his senior yearbook, under his picture, the class had elected him least likely to succeed. What they actually wrote under his picture were these words: HE'LL NEVER AMOUNT TO ANYTHING!

After graduation, Turfy joined his dad's septic tank cleaning business. The cleaning equipment was kept in the back of a converted van. One day, Turfy's dad asked him to redo the badly faded business sign on the side of the truck. Turfy wasn't sure what he should write. His dad told him just to be truthful. "Say what we do and how we do it," the old man explained.

Turfy made a new sign that read, "TURPEINEN'S SEPTIC CLEANING SERVICE. WE'RE NOT CAREFUL BUT WE'RE SLOW." They lost a lot of business after that, but Turfy and his dad didn't mind. The less they had to do, the more time they had to do nothing. "Ah, it's only money!" the old man would say, and Turfy would guffaw at the old man's wisdom.

Turfy liked doing nothing. He was very good at it and could do it for hours. He liked doing nothing in a local coffee shop that specialized in people like Turfy. The place was always full of people who did nothing and had nothing to say. The local patrons were specialists in clichés, especially about the weather. Turfy liked to listen to these people. He imagined himself a collector of clichés. He saw a profound kind of wisdom in statements like these: "If you don't like the weather up here, just wait a minute, and it'll change," or "It's colder 'n a witch's tit out there today."

Turfy tried to memorize all the clichés that he heard in the coffee shop, but he always got them mangled. His favorite was about a horse, but when he tried it out on the waitress, she just looked baffled and then withdrew very rapidly from his table and called over a deputy sheriff, who was drinking coffee at another table. "This man just said something obscene to me," the waitress told the deputy.

The deputy ordered Turfy to repeat what he had said. "You can beat a horse under water, but you can't make him think," said Turfy.

The deputy looked baffled. He asked Turfy to repeat it, so Turfy did. "That doesn't made any sense," said the deputy. Turfy explained that it was a cliché and that he collected them.

Another patron, a regular who had been listening to the conversation, piped up. "He got it all wrong, that's all," he said. "He meant to say that you can lead a horse to water, but you can't make him drink. He never gets anything right. He's thick, you know."

"Sure," said another patron, who had gone to school with Turfy. "When they was givin' out brains, Turfy was behind the door."

"He's dumb as a doorknob," said another.

"Loose as a goose," said a fourth.

"A nut without a bolt," said someone else.

The deputy went back to his coffee. The waitress studiously avoided Turfy's table for the rest of her shift.

In the following days, Turfy's life began to change for the better. The other patrons began to go out of their way to impart their clichéd wisdom to Turfy. They would sit at his table and repeat some trite phrase over and over until Turfy got it right. "Repeat after me," they'd say. "He's dead as a doornail."

Turfy would repeat the phrase until he got it right every time.

Eventually, he possessed just as many clichés as the rest of the shop patrons. He could talk about the weather with the best of them. He was very proud of his new-found knowledge. Eventually, he learned the first names of all the other regulars of the coffee shop. His life was complete. He came in early every morning, said hello to each customer, and recited a cliché. The others threw another cliché back, and Turfy guffawed with delight.

Eventually, Turfy gave up altogether the work with his dad and became a full-time coffee shop hanger-on. He felt fulfilled and happy in his role as a cliché collector. It had become a kind of profession. He felt on the leading edge of things.

He's been on that edge ever since.

Joe Heinonen

Joe Heinonen was a third-generation Finnish-American whose grandfather had come to Hancock at the turn of the century to work in the mines. Joe's father also had been a miner until a falling beam crushed his head. Only eight when his father died, Joe grew up hating mines. He didn't like Hancock much either.

As a boy he spent countless hours looking at pictures in old *National Geographic* magazines and dreaming of places where the biggest excitement each week was not the sermon at the Lutheran Church or the game at the high school.

Joe had a miserable childhood. Teachers and peers noticed only his short stature and his acne. After graduation from high school in 1953, Joe tried to enlist, to see a bit of the world. The Army rejected him because he had some torn back muscles, sustained falling off the shed roof while clearing it of snow. Later, Joe passed the civil service examination to become a letter carrier in the Hancock post office. Soon settled into the routine of his job, Joe sought a wife to add excitement to his nights and companionship to his days. But pretty girls that Joe had noticed from afar in high school had already married or gone south to Green Bay or Detroit to find work.

Gladys Erkkila had not fled Hancock or married. Plain and dumpy, she still lived at home with her parents and clerked in a local hardware store. In high school and afterwards, she had never attracted anybody, but she figured that Joe was so ugly that she had a better than average chance with him. Every day when he delivered mail to her family, Gladys met him at the door. Eventually, he asked her out to a movie, and, a few months later, against his own better judgment, he proposed. He pretended not to care about Gladys' physical flaws—her puffy face, broad hips, and solid legs. He also pretended not to care about her lack of curiosity and imagination.

Several times during their engagement, Joe tried to tell Gladys about his dreams of visiting distant lands. Gladys always changed the subject to something less foreign—a dress seen in a shop window or a casserole recipe recently tried.

After their marriage, Joe remained a letter carrier for fifteen years. Every morning, he rose at six-thirty, breakfasted on toast and coffee while Gladys slept in and walked the quarter mile to the central post office to pick up his route mail. He finished sorting by nine and at nine-thirty began deliveries along the west side of Portage Street.

Joe had plenty of time to think as he moved from house to house. Many thoughts were bitter. He wondered why there was little love in his marriage, why he and Gladys had no children, why he felt displaced in the community he'd called home all his life.

After fifteen years, Joe became uncontrollably restless. He worried often about his heart and began to suffer frequent stomach pains. His doctor diagnosed nerves and recommended a new hobby. Joe began to frequent the public library, to read books about distant places. He became obsessed with seeing the world before he died. Joe—only thirty-five—thought constantly about dying. Day after day, he harped at Gladys, threatening to leave her. Gladys, belittling Joe's restlessness, fed him aspirin in coffee.

Joe could stand stifling quietude no longer. In 1971, he planned an itinerary. He sneaked fifteen hundred dollars from their savings and bought a plane ticket. He would take a flight west to San Francisco and across the Pacific to Asia.

The night before he was to leave, Joe told Gladys his plans. Gladys, mortified, wondered what had gone wrong.

"I'll tell you, Gladys," Joe said, "you have to take me seriously. I'm leaving on tomorrow's plane for San Francisco."

"Sure," Gladys replied with false joviality. "It'll be just like last time."

"What are you talking about?" asked Joe. "I haven't ever run away before this. I've only talked about it."

"Sure you did," said Gladys. "The night after you proposed, you tried to run away to Green Bay. That was a long time ago, but I've never forgotten. I'd told all my friends about our engagement, and you almost ruined everything. You sat in the bus station for an hour before you got some sense in your thick head and came back."

"That was different," Joe said. "I was just a kid then—not a mature man."

"Sure," said Gladys, crossing and uncrossing beefy legs. "You're getting old, Joe. I know what's on your mind. Just like all men your age, you want one last chance to sleep with young girls. It isn't me who's slowing down in bed, Joe. You don't seem to want to sleep with me anymore. Stop and think about it. It's you, too. It's too bad we never had a baby."

"That isn't it at all," said Joe. "You'll never understand."

"Sure," said Gladys.

❈   ❈   ❈   ❈   ❈

Joe's flight stopped briefly on Guam to refuel. After leaving Guam, Joe slept until the harsh crackle of the plane's intercom announced that the flight had entered Vietnamese air space and would soon be over Cambodia. Now wide awake, Joe examined night sky outside his window and was surprised to see many blinking lights. Down below, the earth erupted into roiling mounds of orange flame. After several minutes, Joe realized that the orange mounds were exploding bombs and that the distant blinking lights were high-flying bombers.

As Joe stared out at the blossoming orange flowers of death, the stewardess pulled out his plastic tray and left a steak dinner and cocktail. Joe, very hungry, ate the steak with zest. Nearby, a businessman in a conservative dark suit slumbered loudly, withdrawn breath bubbling out of his nostrils. Across the aisle, a little boy had discovered the furious orange fire. He pulled several times on his mother's arm. "The television has fireworks on it," squealed the child with delight. "It's just like the Fourth of July, Mommy."

The mother was reading a magazine and refused to be disturbed. She ignored the child until he pulled on her arm the third time. Then she slapped his fingers. Licking at the pain, the child turned back to the little round window to peer into the darkness.

When the stewardess came along the aisle to collect food trays and plastic glasses, Joe asked her about the bombing. "Do you often fly this route at night?" he asked.

"Of course," she replied. "I've flown this route many times."

"Are they always bombing?" he asked. "And whose side are they on—ours or theirs?"

"I don't know what you're talking about," she replied as she dumped the food tray and cup into a plastic sack.

"I can see huge bubbles of orange flame out there," Joe said as he motioned toward the window.

"We just passed over an electrical storm," explained the stewardess. "You must have seen some lightning. You have nothing to worry about. We're flying high above the storm and won't begin our descent for some time yet." The stewardess threw Joe a penetrating smile and moved up the aisle.

Still curious, Joe pushed his face against the glass and searched the darkness for more explosions. The fire storm was over. Far away, he could detect the soft blink of lights. Soon they were gone.

✿   ✿   ✿   ✿   ✿

The petite doll-women in the floating brothel of Bangkok stood in line in the bows of tiny sampans, one girl to one boat. Each girl extended a diminutive leg through a split skirt. Customers passed slowly down the line to make deliberate choices. When the haggling was completed and the customer had climbed into the boat, the old lady in the stern revved the engine and steered into mid-channel of the canal. The old woman cut the engine and waited silently while the sampan rocked gently to the rhythm of love.

Joe stood on the outer edge of the crowd of customers, pimps, and hangers-on. He watched the others pass back and forth before the prostitutes. Joe stood there all afternoon, waiting expectantly for something to happen. Nothing did.

✿   ✿   ✿   ✿   ✿

On the plane to Katmandu, Joe sat behind an American couple in their eighties. The couple wore identical flowered shirts and sandals. As the plane soared through a narrow cleft in the Himalayas, the old lady turned to Joe. "Young man," she said in a high-pitched, quavering voice, "can I ask you a question?"

"Certainly," said Joe.

"Do you know where we are?"

"Sure," replied Joe. "We're over the Himalayas on our way to Katmandu."

"Where?"

"Katmandu," Joe repeated.

"Where's that?" the old lady asked.

"It's in Central Asia," Joe said patiently.

"What's he say?" the old man shouted to his wife, who sat right beside him. Apparently he was deaf.

"He says we're somewhere in Asia," the old lady shouted.

"Can't be," the old man shouted back. "Ev'ry blamed place we've been for a week they've said was Asia."

"Asia is a big place," said Joe.

"What'd he say?" the old man shouted.

"He says Asia's a big place," shouted his wife.

"Huh!" snorted the old man in vexation. "New York. That's big. This Asia place it ain't nothin' but dirt and filth."

"Katmandu is supposed to be pretty," Joe said.

"You been to New York?" the old man shouted huffily.

"No, sir," replied Joe.

"You go there," the old man shouted, his voice ringing sharply with command. "That's big. This Asia ain't nothin'. Dirt and filth."

Embarrassed, Joe turned from the old couple to stare out the window. Massive, cloud-swept peaks of the world's highest mountains cut sharp angles into the surrounding sky.

✻   ✻   ✻   ✻   ✻

In Katmandu, Joe joined a young French woman named Françoise for an excursion across the valley floor in a rusty bus packed with peasants. After touring the world's largest stupa, she and Joe climbed on foot through terraced fields toward the foothills of the Himalayas. En route, they stopped briefly to rest in the shade of a mud-brick home. A beautiful young mother hovered in the slatted shadow of her doorway. Joe wanted to entice the woman into the yard, to see her face against the majestic backdrop of mountains. Instead, the woman sent out her daughter to beg. The daughter circled with shy sidesteps until Joe gave her some rupees. The girl clutched the coins tightly and scurried away. On the farmhouse wall were huge pancakes of cow dung, slapped there to dry for fuel.

Higher in the foothills, Françoise became dizzy from the rarefied air. She and Joe rested under a wind-bent tree. Françoise had long bangs that fell in her eyes. She wore frayed blue jeans and sherpa boots. She promised to stay with Joe while he was in Katmandu, as long as he agreed to pay for whatever she desired. She believed in the liberation of women but not of men. "You men always seem to enjoy sex more than we do," she said, "so you should continue to pay for it." She had slept with more than one hundred men since leaving France on a pilgrimage to the birthplace of the Gautama. She was happy in Nepal and never wished to return to France, where she had labored as a cashier in a fashionable Parisian boutique.

Joe was afraid Françoise would spend a lot of his money if he gave her the opportunity. Also, her blatant sexuality terrified him. He told her he wasn't sure he could afford her. She laughed and said he was an enjoyable old fool.

On the way out of the hills, Françoise met a young adventurer from Wichita. Joe never saw her again.

❖   ❖   ❖   ❖   ❖

Hotel keepers in Tehran had a slow and easy charm. They were very helpful and treated a foreigner with patience. The young guides were often students, buoyant with optimism that oil money and revolution had brought. They took no money for services and insisted that they only wished to practice English. They all seemed to have relatives in America, studying at various universities. Some guides wished to study in America, also, but none wished to live there. They all felt times were good in Iran, and they wished to grow with the country.

Joe wondered about continuing turmoil. When he asked guides whether or not there were many political prisoners, they refused to answer and walked away.

❖   ❖   ❖   ❖   ❖

In Eastern Turkey, men in pancake hats and jodhpurs fingered worry beads and smoked incessantly as the overladen bus droned up and down the barren, rock-strewn land. At each arid hilltop, a man would descend. From his seat, Joe watched each farmer stretch cramped muscles beside the dust-laden road before seeking the meager shade of stunted trees. As he stretched, each man carefully surveyed the cultivated fields of poppies.

The quiet stoicism of the poppy farmers irritated Joe. "Someone ought to do something," he said aloud to no one in particular. "The land ought to be condemned. Next year some kid in New York will die from an overdose of heroin grown right here."

Everyone on the bus grew silent. Joe glanced around and noticed others staring. He slouched quietly into his seat. *They must think I'm mad,* he thought. *A stranger talking to himself about things he doesn't understand. Here I sit, judging poor farmers who own virtually nothing. We all judge. Man judges the earth and God judges man. Gladys judges too. She's judging right now. She'll judge me after I'm home, and she won't forget. There's no justice in it, but it's a truth.*

❖   ❖   ❖   ❖   ❖

When Joe Heinonen reached Istanbul, he had a sour stomach. He located aspirin in a small shop near his hotel, but the shopkeeper could not speak English. When Joe left the shop, he tried to find a decent cup of coffee, but everywhere the Turks gave him a tiny cup of something that tasted like mud. Eventually, he gave up in disgust and took a taxi to the airport. The next day, he flew to New York. His stomach still hurt.

❖   ❖   ❖   ❖   ❖

The day after that Joe returned to Hancock. He got his old job back. Inside he felt peculiarly calm, almost as if he were dead. Gladys seemed delighted that he had returned. She had talked the people at the post office into holding his job. With their normal life again intact, Gladys wanted to celebrate. She called over the neighbors, the Toivolas, to share coffee and cake. The Toivolas, like Joe, were third-generation Finnish-Americans.

"So, you're back!" exclaimed Mr. Toivola as he came through the door to slap Joe affectionately on the back.

"Sure," replied Joe.

"So, how was the trip?" asked Mrs. Toivola with strained cheerfulness.

"Fine," said Joe.

"Did you get to Helsinki?" asked Mr. Toivola, his smile stretching broadly. "It's a beautiful city, isn't it?"

"I don't know," said Joe. "I just went across Asia."

"You spent all that money, and you never went to Finland?" Mr. Toivola asked in disbelief. "I guess I just assumed that's where you went."

"Mr. Toivola and I were there about ten years ago," said Mrs. Toivola. "It was sort of a delayed honeymoon. It was really something."

"Sure," said Mr. Toivola. "Really something. If a fella's going to go anywhere, he ought to go back to the old country."

"Well, where did you go?" asked Mrs. Toivola suspiciously.

"Asia," replied Joe. "Bangkok, Katmandu, Tehran, Istanbul."

"Leave it to Joe to go places nobody's ever heard of," said Gladys.

"Well, at least he's back now," said Mrs. Toivola, "so you can rest easy, Gladys."

"Oh, I'm happy to have him back," said Gladys as she squeezed Joe's shoulder. "I was afraid some sweet young thing might've run off with him."

"No girl could take Joe away from his Gladys for long," laughed Mr. Toivola. "Seriously, though, why didn't you go to Helsinki while you were over there?"

"I never thought of it," replied Joe.

"I would have gone to Paris, France, if I had my druthers," said Gladys, "but, of course, he didn't ask me."

"At least we've heard of that," said Mrs. Toivola. "You could've brought Gladys some nice perfume. What did he bring you, Gladys? A shrunken head?"

"Nothing at all," replied Gladys, hurt by the question. "But that doesn't matter. All I really wanted was Joe."

"Isn't that sweet?" Mrs. Toivola said, addressing Joe.

Joe said nothing.

"Why did you go to those places?" Mr. Toivola asked, but without waiting for a reply, he added, "I'll bet the people smelled!"

"I don't know," said Joe. "I didn't notice."

"Oh, I would have noticed," exclaimed Mrs. Toivola. "I always notice. That's why I hate crowds."

"We should go into the living room," said Gladys. "I made a chocolate cake, and the coffee is perking."

"That sounds wonderful, Gladys," said Mr. Toivola. "I love that cake of yours."

"Mr. Toivola is always raving about that cake of yours," Mrs. Toivola said. "I guess I'll have to get the recipe, Gladys."

Gladys smiled broadly.

"Next time," added Mr. Toivola, addressing Joe.

"What?" said Joe.

"Helsinki," said Mr. Toivola.

Uncle Leon

Matti Leinonen and his Lapp wife, Liisa, emigrated from Vaasa, Finland, to the Upper Peninsula in 1905. Matti worked in the copper mines, but his true vocation was farming. He eventually saved enough money to buy a rock-strewn farm in the Traprock Valley. He and Liisa built themselves a log farmhouse and a barn in 1912 and moved there with their six children. The oldest child, Lemppi, who had been born in Finland, died in an automobile accident in her teens, while she was on her way to Detroit to seek employment as a maid. The second oldest, Aina, married an abusive husband when she was sixteen. She had a series of nervous breakdowns in her twenties, and, by thirty years of age, she was permanently ensconced in the state hospital for the insane. The third oldest, Toivo, drank himself to death at a young age. The fourth oldest, Eija, married an illiterate miner who could barely speak English and whose Finnish was equally rudimentary. Every weekend, Eija and her husband got drunk and abused each other physically and verbally. The hopes of the family fell to the two youngest children.

Wilbert was a normal son. He fished and hunted as a boy, helped his father on the farm, and took care of the cows, chickens, and horses. He finished the seventh grade and then built himself a boat, fished Lake Superior, and peddled the catch door to door from Hancock to South Range. By the time he was in his twenties, he was a successful businessman with a second, larger boat and a crew. He sold his fish out of a small shop in Hancock. During the off season, he made good money plowing roads for the county and doing whatever odd jobs came his way.

The youngest of Matti and Liisa's children, Leon, appeared to be a normal Finn when, at the age of eight, he took to coffee as if it were the staff of life. From then to the end of his life, he drank between twenty and thirty cups a day. Other than that, he was weird. He was the only Finn in the history of the world who totally lacked *sisu*.

As a small child, he was a mama's boy, hanging onto Liisa's apron. He grew up to become a whimpering little boy-man, terrified of almost everything. He suffered from an overwhelming fear of closed-in spaces. Maybe his claustrophobia came from his Lapp blood—blood that was only at home on the great open spaces of the tundra. Whatever the reason, Leon was the only miner in the Copper Country with an acute case of claustrophobia. While other miners wore hard hats to protect themselves from falling rocks and broken timbers, Leon wore his because he was sure that, at any moment, an entire mountain was going to crash down on his head. The other miners teased him about his affliction. "Dammit, Leon," they'd say, "you live in the Midwest. There's no mountain on top of this mine."

"Maybe not," Leon would reply, "but if this thing ever caves in, it'll feel like a mountain."

Leon remained a miner for a surprising number of years, but, in 1936, he took his ax and crosscut and went into the Hiawatha National Forest to log. He could only bear logging for a few years. All those trees closed him in, disoriented him, and made his nose bleed.

He tried the sawmill, but the constant whine of the saws, the clouds of fine wood dust, and the burned smell when the saws hit a large knot drove him wild with fear.

By the time World War II began, Leon had decided there was definitely something wrong with Finns. "They always choose to live in cold and uncomfortable places—like Finland and the Upper Peninsula," he said. "They also believe in a strict work ethic, in the spiritual value of hard, physical labor. They are idiots!"

In 1945, the *Enola Gay* dropped an atomic bomb on Hiroshima and ended the work ethic for about 70,000 Japanese. That event ended the working days for Leon, too. He decided to quit the sawmill and just be. "Nothing makes sense anyway," he said. He withdrew to his parents' farm, never to leave it to go to work again. He began to tell visitors to the farm that a version of the *Enola Gay* lurked somewhere in the forest behind the farm. "It looks like a silver bird. It sails out of the darkness in the middle of the night, floats in through my bedroom window, and sits with terrible force right on the top of my head."

Leon's father, Matti, died of a stroke in the fall of 1946. That Christmas, his mother, Liisa, visited friends on a nearby farm. The friends and she got drunk on vodka. Liisa left to return home well past midnight. She reached the farm, but Leon had accidentally locked her out while he snoozed by the kitchen wood stove. She beat on the door several minutes, and then curled up on the porch and fell asleep. Snow drifted over her. When Leon awakened two hours later and went looking for her, he found her huddled into a tight ball. He brought her inside by the fire, but her feet were frozen. Except for threads of blue, they were dead white, like pieces of alabaster with blue trim. Leon stoked the fire, left her and went to get his brother, Wilbert. Wilbert called the doctor. When the doctor, Wilbert, and Leon reached the farm, Liisa was screaming with pain as her flesh thawed. The doctor gave her shots and took her away. The next day, at the hospital, he cut off her toes and part of each foot. After that, Liisa walked only with the help of crutches or a walker. In the summer of 1947, she too died of a stroke.

Leon lived on, alone, at the farm. Wilbert supplied him with food, clothing, and other necessities and paid the property taxes. He became a kind of one-man welfare system that supplied all Leon's basic wants. Leon became more and more eccentric. He became obsessed with the European holocaust and the horrors of the German concentration camps. He began to call himself a poor Lutheran Jew. He kept a pitchfork within easy reach by the front door and used it as a mild threat whenever any visitor approached the farm.

The farm itself became terribly rundown. With each passing year, the farmhouse leaned more and more precariously toward the nearby road. Leon propped logs against the jutting wall to slow imminent collapse. The front porch split from the doorway. Exterior walls lost all semblance of paint. Clapboards fell away. Glassless windows rotted at the frames. Some roofing flapped wildly whenever the wind gusted. The broken-backed barn bulged with moldy hay and countless mice. The barn's main floor was littered with outdated field tools and animal harnesses. A once thriving apple orchard was now half dead, the fruit misshapen and wormy. The yard was overgrown with thistles and matted hay. Stands of poplar reclaimed the fields.

Wilbert brought Leon half a dozen cans of red paint and asked him to repaint the house. After Wilbert left, Leon opened all six cans with a pocket knife. With a wicked war whoop, he sailed the first can toward the barn. The can thwacked against weathered boards, leaving a huge, bleeding blotch. Soon the front wall of the barn was decorated with five bleeding blotches. Red streaks slithered down the wall to form sticky puddles on the ground.

Leon didn't throw the last can. He reclosed it and walked into town. At the hardware store, he traded in the red for pink. Then he returned to the farm, located an ancient paintbrush, and painted pink skulls and crossbones on trees bordering his land and on the front side of the house. He wrote DANGER! on one tree and MINED! WATCH OUT! on another. He was about to write HIGH VOLTAGE on a third, when he finally remembered what people usually wrote. After that, he wrote NO TRESPASSING in hot pink letters a foot high on the remainder of the trees. On the side of the house, he wrote HOTEL. "I should have gotten black," he told himself, as he surveyed his completed work.

As the farmhouse deteriorated over the years and as each winter brought cold that advanced farther and farther into the interior of the house, Leon eventually found himself living only in the pantry. He had a chair, a cot, and a wood stove in there. He'd sit by the stove all winter like a hibernating animal. By spring, his uncut and unkempt hair was coated with granular soot. So was his skin. His clothes were unspeakably filthy. Whenever Wilbert brought Leon food and drink, Leon would rave about the walls of the pantry—that they were closing in on him and suffocating him. Leon began to pray that someone would tarmac the entire Upper Peninsula and turn it all into one big parking lot. "Then nothing could fall on my head but the sky," said Leon.

Each April, Leon waited for a rare, bright warm day to make a trip into town. He would arrive at Wilbert's boat dock just as Wilbert brought in the day's catch of trout and whitefish. Wilbert always had a fifth of vodka waiting on the boat. He'd hand it to Leon, who would pour the contents down his throat in one fell stream of liquid fire. Soon Leon would be in a stupor. Wilbert and his crewmen would peel off Leon's sooty clothes and drop them off the end of the dock. Then Wilbert and the others would pour a bottle of Lestoil over Leon's head, and, as the liquid ran down his soot-blackened body, they'd rub him down. When Leon glowed with an oily coat, Wilbert and his crewmen would toss Leon off the end of the dock into Portage Lake. Leon would rise up sputtering after the icy shock. He would boom out Finnish blasphemies that would echo through Hancock streets. Then Wilbert would hand Leon clean used clothes from St. Vinnie's. Leon would put them on and then mount to the deckhouse roof of Wilbert's boat. "Listen to my call!" he would shout to anyone who had come to watch his spring cleaning. "I have been baptized by the good hands of the fisherman. My brothers and sisters, I am saved! Come to me now, you sinning townspeople! Come to me and you too can be saved! Let me throw you, with or without garments, into the cleansing grip of the icy waters!"

No one ever came forward for salvation. Soon Leon would trudge back to his farm, alone and isolated.

On mild summer Sundays Leon toppled birches from other people's land and cut them into manageable short logs to be hand-carried back to his farm. Balancing a log on his shoulders, he staggered down the center of the highway. He moved to the side of the road and let local traffic pass, but tourist traffic had to wait until he reached the farm. Sometimes, just to irritate somebody from downstate, he dropped his burden across the road and sat on it while he smoked his pipe. For no particular reason, Leon hated tourists. He called him flatlanders, trolls, or downstaters, and, sometimes, when he was in an extra foul mood, he just called them "those bastards from Detroit." He wondered aloud sometimes why they persecuted him so, condemning him "to wander forever the confines of a worthless and rock-strewn damned farm."

Eventually, Leon's erratic behavior began to bother the neighbors. When surveyors came through to prepare for a widening of the road, he drove them off his land with his pitchfork. A man from Detroit bought a wood lot adjacent to the farm one fall and planned to come north the following summer to build himself a camp there. In the intervening months, Leon cut down all the salable trees on the man's lot and sold the wood to a local trucker who pretended he didn't know whose wood it was. "I thought it was Leon's," the trucker told the sheriff. In the end, the sheriff didn't do anything except to tell Wilbert to keep an eye on Leon. "If he does something like that to a local person, I'll have to take action," the sheriff said.

The locals forgave Leon's eccentricities in the early spring of 1956. On a windy April day, Leon stepped over the last remaining drifts of snow and strode onto open shoreline of a fishing pond. At that moment, a boat flipped over in choppy waves, throwing three fishermen in heavy clothes into the water. Leon kicked off his boots and then tore off soot-laden layers of sweaty coats, sweaters, flannel shirts, long johns, and wool pants and dove into the water. He rescued two men who were unable to swim in their heavy clothes. The third fisherman clung to the boat and floated ashore. Leon stripped layers of soaked clothing from the men and wrapped them in his own fetid but dry clothes. Soon he had a fire roaring.

As the men huddled around the fire, the warmth began to bring out the odor of Leon's clothes in full force. One fisherman complained that if he'd had his druthers, he would have rather drowned than be sitting there wrapped in the overpowering stink of Leon's yellowed and browned long johns. "Stink!" shouted Leon. "How can you complain about the stink when you've been rescued by a naked, wandering, Lutheran Jew?"

As he grew older, Leon mellowed. He rarely suffered from wild emotional outbursts. A mythology about his powers as a Finnish healer and singer came into existence from unknown quarters. In actuality, Leon could not carry a tune, and the only songs he knew were a few Lutheran hymns, including "Dragging Her Out of the Swamp," an odd but sacrosanct piece only sung on St. Urho's Day by the boys in the Mosquito Inn.

In the spring of 1959, Leon came into town for his annual bath. He drank his usual fifth of vodka, and, as usual, Wilbert and the others befouled the waters at the end of the dock with Leon's filthy clothes. A moment later they had soaped him up and had pushed him into the icy waters. At that moment, a playful speedboat full of tourists came roaring past the dock in a tight arc. Wilbert tried to wave the boat away, but the boat cut sharply in, as if the occupants were curious to see what was transpiring. The speed tossed a black wing of water onto Wilbert and the other men as the boat sped by. An instant later, Wilbert heard a dull rasping, as if someone had tossed a handful of gravel into the path of the prop.

Wilbert dove in and pulled out Leon, who had a three-inch gash from behind his right ear to the top of his head. A clump of his hair was missing.

After that, it was all downhill for Leon. The doctors who examined him and sewed him up at the hospital decided that he should not return to the farm. "His living conditions are too harsh," they said. The fire department razed the farm after the township declared it a hazard. "We don't want our kids going over there and getting bitten by a rodent or getting crushed by a falling building," neighbors said.

Wilbert didn't know what else to do, so he signed the papers that put Leon in the state hospital for the insane. "At least he'll be with family," said Wilbert, referring to Aina, who, by then, had been in the hospital for longer than Wilbert could remember exactly.

Leon liked almost everything about the hospital "except the crazy people." He quickly fell into a routine typical of old Finnish men from the Upper Peninsula. He had a small but powerful radio by his bed, and, every day from spring to early fall, he'd listen religiously to Detroit Tigers' games. From fall to winter, he'd listen to Lions' games, and from winter to spring to Red Wings' games. The Pistons had only recently moved to Detroit from Fort Wayne and were not yet worthy of deification. Of the holy sports trinity, Leon much preferred baseball. "It's the only thing in life that makes sense," he told Wilbert during a visitation.

On October 1, 1961, at the precise moment when Roger Maris stroked his sixty-first home run into the right field stands of Yankee Stadium, which, simultaneously, was the precise moment when Norm Cash finished the season as a Tiger with a league-leading .361 batting average, Leon died of a stroke. He had just consumed his two-hundred-thousandth cup of strong, black coffee. In Old Finnish Man terms, he had about as perfect a death as one could have. Wilbert saw to it that Leon was buried above ground in a cement mausoleum with a large picture window. Leon probably didn't know the difference, but Wilbert did. Sometimes Wilbert visits the grave to clean the window with Windex. After all, Leon hated being closed in.

Isaac Tikkanen

Peter Tikkanen grew up in a fanatically ultra-conservative family that attended the Old Apostolic Lutheran Church. Peter's parents disapproved of most other Apostolics because they were too liberal. Some of those other families subscribed to newspapers, or the wives read Harlequin romances, or the husbands read the *National Enquirer*, or they showed their corruption in some other way. Peter's family lived miles from town on a back road inhabited only by them and their relatives. They and their relatives associated only with each other.

Peter's mother wore long dresses and kept her hair in a bun. She made sure that her children were in church every week, and she protected them from all signs of the devil at work in the world. Peter and his fifteen siblings saw no television, heard no rock music, read no books or magazines not approved ahead of time by Pastor Kinnunen. The kids drank no alcohol, spoke to no secular humanists, ate plain foods, and prayed a lot. Fifty percent of the walls in the home and one hundred percent of the books contained pictures of Jesus. Occasionally, they were allowed to read the *Reader's Digest*.

In school, Peter and his many siblings did their civic duty by passing their courses with good grades. They also did their religious duty by disregarding all knowledge that even remotely challenged what they already knew with certainty to be true—that they and people like themselves were predestined to join the handful of other righteous ones who would one day sit on the right hand of God in heaven.

When Peter reached his teens, he began to work in the woods full time, and he began to smoke Marlboros because the Bible said nothing directly against it. He began to lust a lot in his heart. Actually, he thought about sex pretty much all the time when he wasn't praying and a good

114

share of the time when he was.

Shortly after his eighteenth birthday, Peter married Ruth, a member of Peter's congregation. Ruth was also from a fanatically ultra-conservative family. She was sixteen. The immediate families and their relatives built Peter and Ruth a home and sauna just down the road from Peter's parents' place and not far from the homes of Peter's many aunts, uncles, great-aunts, great-uncles, cousins, brothers, sisters, and grandparents. As a wedding present, Peter and Ruth received a big van. "You'll need it when you start to produce children," they were told.

Peter and Ruth discovered on their wedding night that they really enjoyed the religious duty of trying to produce righteous children for the Lord. They'd just get done doing it once when, lo and behold, they'd want to do it again. They had always been very religious, but never in their lives had they been so fulfilled in their duty.

Sometimes during the day, Peter would come home from his logging out in the woods, and they'd do it again during lunch.

At night, they'd often lie abed and discuss the future—when the Archangel would sweep down out of heaven and carry them, their many future children, their relatives, and the few other righteous ones up to Heaven while everyone else suffered from God's wrath. Sometimes they'd add up all of their righteous relatives (being sure to leave out their Uncle Toivo, who spent way too much time in the bars in Hancock) and all the other righteous members of their parish and then all the righteous relatives of those parish members, and they'd come up with an astoundingly large figure. "When you come right down to it, Heaven is going to be more or less full of our relatives and friends and fellow ultra-conservative Old Church Apostolics," Peter would say with pride and wonder, and Ruth would smile with happiness and relief, for she didn't like the idea of having to spend even one minute of eternity with members of those other Apostolic sects or with folks from the Missouri Synod, the Wisconsin Synod, or, God forbid, the LCA. She knew for a fact that some of those Lutheran groupings contained non-Finn Lutherans, and that idea horrified her. An eternity with Catholics, Baptists, and Buddhists was absolutely out of the question!

Sometimes there in bed, just before or just after they'd tried once again to produce a righteous child for the Lord, Peter and Ruth would wonder why Heaven was apparently reserved for Old Church Apostolics and, therefore, for Finns. Did God speak Finnish? Peter wondered. Such questions were dangerous since they had been taught never to question the ways of God. They supposed that He did, however.

Peter wondered what kind of seat they would have on the right hand of God. He said he would opt for a La-Z-Boy if he had a choice in the matter. Ruth said she'd prefer some sort of antique chair—a blue one.

Peter and Ruth sometimes discussed current events. Their two sources of information were Pastor Kinnunen's Sunday sermons and religious radio broadcasts. They knew about the rising tide of crime, illegitimacy, and divorce in the country, and they thought it was wonderful. The growing evil meant that Armageddon was at hand and that they would soon be in Heaven. Neither Peter nor Ruth had any sympathy for criminals. They believed in an eye for an eye. "If somebody commits murder, then he should be murdered," Ruth said. "If the murderer tortured his victim, then he, too, should be tortured." Peter wholeheartedly agreed.

"But what if the police or witnesses made a mistake, and they execute the wrong man?" Peter asked one night.

"It doesn't matter," Ruth said. "Let God sort them out."

Both Peter and Ruth were quite sure that the chance of any of those people reaching Heaven was pretty slim anyway. "Unless they are Old Church people like us," said Ruth.

Ruth frequently mentioned how happy she was that the Lord had made her a holy vessel to produce more righteous children to fill up Heaven. "He's given us such wonderful power," she said, and then her hand would wander down Peter's body to the seat of that power. A moment later, they would be at it again.

A little over nine months later, Isaac was born. Ruth was overcome with the wonder of his birth and showered him with love. So did Peter. "The power of God is in him," Ruth would say as Isaac slept peacefully at the foot of their bed.

"And in us," Peter would add.

"And in our love," Ruth would add.

"He's given us this power," Peter would say.

"And we ought to use it," Ruth would say, and her hand would wander.

✿ ✿ ✿ ✿ ✿

On a frigid January Saturday night, when little Isaac was not quite one and a half, Ruth, now pregnant with her second child, drove into town to get herself the cigarettes that Peter had forgotten to buy earlier in the day. Peter, worn out from a long day of stacking wood, plowing snow, and repairing a tractor, slept curled up in front of the wood stove in the living room.

Outside, the wind moaned through the trees and gusted against the house, shivering the shingles. The lonely road into town sparkled with a layer of moonlit ice. The temperature hovered well below zero.

On the return from town, the Tikkanen van skidded out of a turn and slammed into a snowbank. Ruth cracked five ribs on the steering wheel. She left the half-buried van to begin a painful two-mile walk to her home. Her cracked ribs made every step an ordeal. Soon the journey became a battle for survival against the violent cold. For some reason that Peter later could not comprehend, she passed by an aunt's house without seeking help.

Peter woke hours later, stoked the stove, waited nervously a few minutes, and then rushed outside to scan the road. Moments later, he hurried toward town, frightened by the sharp gusts of wind and the snap of frost under his feet. The icy air bit his lungs.

Peter found his wife huddled against a snowbank, a hundred yards from their home. She was frozen blue. He carried her home and tried to thaw her out near the stove, but she was gone. Disbelieving, he heated water and wrapped her icy body in dripping towel compresses. Soon a steaming puddle spread across the floor and under the stove. Peter was too distraught to notice. He sat all night on the edge of a chair, staring in disbelief at his marble wife. At dawn he roused Isaac, wrapped him warmly, and carried him to the aunt's home. Then he went for a doctor.

For months afterwards, Peter rarely spoke. For the first time in his life, he began to drink. He joined his Uncle Toivo in Hancock's bars. He began to swear a great deal and forgot to wash. Occasionally, he sobered up enough to cut a little wood to sell for food and beer money. He and Isaac's home grew increasingly filthy and then fell into disrepair. Peter's many relatives tried to console him but without success. When Pastor Kinnunen came for a visit, Peter attacked him with a pitchfork, forcing him back into his car and down the road. Little Isaac, left alone much of the day, ate cold beans from the can and licked peanut butter from a knife. In the evening, Peter sometimes raved to himself while Isaac crouched silently in a corner.

✤   ✤   ✤   ✤   ✤

Eventually, Peter stopped drinking, but he refused to come to terms with God or his grief. He refused to accept the early deaths of his wife and unborn child. Peter's parents and siblings tried to reason with him. All of them said the same thing. "It was a good act—God's act. Now they are in Heaven. Their deaths were part of God's plan. You must have faith in God and in His wisdom."

Peter reacted angrily. "I believe in God," he said, "but I will never agree with His damned plan."

Peter's mother begged him not to curse.

"I'm not cursing," Peter replied. "I'm just stating the truth. God's plan is damned. It's hellish."

Peter's mother told him not to say such things. "It's an abomination," she said. "To war with God is to war with yourself. To show disrespect to God is to show disrespect for yourself."

Peter ordered her and the others out of his house. Her words had made him even angrier since they seemed to make sense.

After they left, Peter called a real estate agent and arranged for the sale of his land. "I have one stipulation," he said to the agent. "The buyer must not be Old Church Apostolic."

The agent was baffled by this request.

"I want my folks' faith tested," said Peter. "The buyer must be Catholic or Baptist or any denomination other than Apostolic. The buyer can even be Lutheran Church of America in a pinch."

Then Peter dressed Isaac and carried the boy out to the van. He returned and sloshed gasoline from a five-gallon can all over the downstairs floor. He emptied the can of its last few drops by the front door. He dug a packet of matches from his jeans, selected one, lit it, and dropped it into the liquid. Flames leaped up and shot across the hardwood floor. Peter watched for a moment, realized that the house and its furnishings would be an inferno within minutes, turned and ran to the van.

Peter drove fast without looking back. Isaac played with a toy on the van floor.

Peter found a furnished house for rent in Coppertown. He also found ready employment at a series of logging operations, and he set out to cut down every tree in God's creation. He viewed his chain saw as a kind of theological weapon. He spent hours every evening polishing and oiling the machine. He spent little time with Isaac because the boy reminded him of Ruth. While Peter was at work, Isaac stayed with a neighbor woman.

About two years after his wife's death, Peter visited Coppertown's tiny library under the stairwell in the firehouse. "Are you the librarian?" he asked the pretty young Finnish woman who sat at the only desk, surrounded by books that smelled of mildew.

"Yes, I am," she said. "Can I help you?"

"Are you Mrs. Annukka Jarvi?" Peter asked.

She told him that she was.

"Does your husband work as a yarder at the pulp mill?"

Mrs. Jarvi admitted that he did.

"Good. I talked to your husband. I cut for the mill. He and I sometimes eat lunch together when I've brought in a load. He said that you and he are members of the Lutheran Church of America."

"Yes, we are," said Mrs. Jarvi.

"Good," said Peter. "Then you know how to help me. I'm looking for the most unGodly book there is. I don't want a library copy. I just want the title and how I can obtain it."

Mrs. Jarvi admitted that she was familiar with a number of books that could fall into the category of being unGodly. "I figured you LCA people would be," said Peter.

"What do you want such a book for?" Mrs. Jarvi asked.

"I have my reasons, but reading it isn't one," said Peter.

Mrs. Jarvi smiled. "I can give you two titles and the addresses of the publishers."

"That would be fine. Thank you," said Peter.

Peter sent directly to the publishers for fifty copies of each book. When the two compact but very heavy cartons arrived by mail two weeks later on a Friday, Peter put them in the back of his van. He left the cartons there until four a.m. on Sunday morning. Then he drove to the Old Apostolic Church, jimmied open the back door and carried the cartons inside.

Next he removed every hymnal from each pew and carried them to the van. He replaced each hymnal either with a copy of Jean Paul Sartre's *Being and Nothingness* or with Henry Miller's *Tropic of Cancer.*

Peter returned home before dawn. That was the last time he ever visited the church.

He burned the hymnals in the wood stove in the kitchen of the rented house. They generated little heat.

✿　　✿　　✿　　✿　　✿

When Isaac came of age, Peter sent him off to school. For a few years, Isaac liked school. He was the first in his class in reading. He discovered that he loved books and could not read enough of them. Soon, however, he found school almost unbearable. He never made any close friends there, and he hated the suffocating regimentation of the classroom. Although the work came easily to him, somehow Isaac never managed to finish it. He found the workbooks horribly repetitive and boring—he couldn't finish a page. Elementary math held no interest. Social Studies was mildly interesting, but he read the year's material in the first three weeks and spent the rest of the year fidgeting or sleeping.

On weekends, Isaac's father invariably made a trip to Houghton to stock up on food, drink, and work necessities at the supermarket or the hardware store. Isaac stayed behind in Coppertown. At such times, he went straight to the town's tiny library to return books and get another week's worth of reading. Mrs. Jarvi recognized Isaac's worth as her best customer and treated him with respect. The library contained all the *National Geographic* magazines from 1912 to the present. During his elementary school years, Isaac set out to read all of them. He also read the books of James Oliver Curwood—a series of novels set in Canada's Northwest Territories. These led to books about Arctic explorers—Scott,

Amundsen, Peary, and Freuchen. Isaac devoured history books, too, but with less avidity. One winter, he read every book he could obtain on Marco Polo and on Genghis Khan.

At school and at home, none of this reading was of much help. His father and the other students simply did not care, and the teachers only cared whether or not Isaac had completed his assignments. By the time Isaac reached the seventh grade, he was considered a hopeless academic and disciplinary case by teachers and supervisors at the school. His father considered him a fool for continuing to attend, although the law said that he must.

✢ ✢ ✢ ✢ ✢

During the fall when Isaac entered high school, Coppertown suffered its first loss in Vietnam—the son of a one-armed logger who sometimes worked with Peter. The boy had joined the Marines right after high school graduation in June. He had returned to Coppertown in late summer. Isaac remembered the boy strutting about town in a starched uniform, bragging incessantly about what he was going to do to "those slant-eyed little jungle bunnies."

In the second month of his Vietnam tour, the boy had been killed by a sniper. Isaac and the other high school students attended the funeral. They were both impressed and depressed by the military ceremony. Among each other, they whispered comments. "He was an arrogant little bastard in that uniform, hey?" someone said. "Where in hell is Vietnam?" asked someone else. "I suppose his old man will spend the insurance money on a new chain saw and truck," a third said.

At Thanksgiving break, Isaac, now fifteen, dropped out of school. Peter got his boy a job driving a pulp truck for the mill. Isaac hated the monotony of the work. Every morning, he drove north into the forest to load. After drinking a beer and eating a bologna sandwich, he headed back to the mill. By night, he had always completed two trips, had eaten lunch, and had reloaded for the next morning. Isaac's only free day was Sunday, when the truck usually needed minor repairs.

Isaac's father had worked twenty years in the woods. He swaggered among the thick hardwood stands, thumping his ready chain saw pridefully against his thigh. "Someday," he'd say to Isaac, "there won't be one damned tree still standing in this state. It's visible progress. Get enough of us together and we'll saw our way clear to Canada—cover this whole state with ranch-houses, swimming pools, the whole works. No more frigging trees and no more shacks."

Peter loved devastating the forest, ripping it apart with his chain saw and the paper company's bulldozer. He'd shout joyously as heavily laden trucks moaned over rude tracks, struggling with logs destined to become Kleenex, toilet paper, or dinner napkins.

Isaac's father loved most of all to combat swarms of black flies that clouded the swamps. When other woodsmen retreated, Peter poured bottles of baby oil over exposed areas of his body and continued to cut. When flies had eaten through the oil, he swept the air with aerosol cans of DDT. "Rat-a-tat-tat!" he'd shout victoriously as the cloud around his head fell to earth.

Isaac could not understand his father, for Isaac hated to see the forest decimated. Isaac also reserved a special hatred for flies, especially for the late June swarms that flooded his nose and ears, forcing him to retreat to his cab. With the cab windows rolled up, he would sit and sip beer while dreaming of life at the South Pole, where there were no insects. His dreams were always short, for there was always work to be done. "Anyway," he muttered to himself, "there aren't any trees down there. I must have trees."

Sometimes Isaac tried to hammer sense into his father's head. "We oughta quit," he said. "We oughta leave these trees to grow and head for Alaska or the top of Canada. We could build ourselves a cabin and live off the land."

"Hell, no!" his father replied. "Cut 'em down! Just like the pioneers!" Then Peter laughed and revved up his saw. "What we *don't* need in the Upper Peninsula is forest and snow. They kill innocent people like your mother. What we *do* need is a big fire to clean out this Peninsula all the way to Canada. I dream of the day when the whole Upper Peninsula is covered with a plastic dome—like they have in Houston. Inside the dome, the plastic grass and the palm trees would always be warm."

❖   ❖   ❖   ❖   ❖

Isaac ignored his mother's grave for most of the year, but, on the night of the anniversary of her wintry death, he always visited it. The graveyard lay in a lonely spot outside Coppertown. After parking his car against the towering snowbank thrown up by the plows, Isaac would struggle through January drifts as if he were trying to swim through thick milk. His mother's grave lay deep under the snow, but, each fall, Isaac marked the spot with an alder stake stuck into the earth at the base of the grave. He always tied a bit of red cloth to the end of the stake. The red cloth was not Isaac's idea. The plowman used similar rude flags to locate mailboxes and other impediments buried along roadways.

Isaac would struggle to the alder stake, line up his body with the grave and fall back, his body striking the drifting snow with a loud whoosh. The impact would entomb most of his body—only the tips of his boots and the circle of his face remaining visible.

On clear nights, Isaac would lie there a long time, staring peacefully into the inky clarity full of stars. On snowy nights, he had to squint to prevent falling flakes from burning his eyes. One year, a blizzard raged, and Isaac had to struggle desperately just to reach the grave. When he lay back, heaven seemed to be falling on his face and suffocating him. The snowflakes were deadly missiles intent on injury.

That night, as the blizzard raged, Isaac tried to think of his mother, but he had no memory of her. He listened to the wind as it howled obscenely past his ears. The small red flag atop the stake vibrated like an outboard engine. Isaac contemplated the darkness out of which the snow blew steadily. He knew that beyond the snow were the planets and beyond them the distant stars of the Milky Way and farther out the empty reaches of space and other galaxies. Isaac had known this since third grade when he had begun to read about the immensity of the universe. Isaac wondered where God was in all this vastness. He asked for a sign—anything that would make him believe. The snow piled up over and around him. "If God won't speak to me, how about you, Martin Luther?" Isaac asked, but the snow just kept falling, and the wind howled viciously. Two hours later, Isaac was shaking with cold, and his soul was sick and empty as he pushed through the storm to reach his car.

A month later, Isaac signed up to be a Marine, and, two months after that, he was in Vietnam. Less than a month into his tour, Isaac dived into an embankment during a firefight, struck his elbow on a rock and fractured his arm into sixteen pieces. After hospitalization and the insertion of a rod into his lower arm, Isaac was declared unfit for combat. He was sent back to the states, to Fort Polk, Louisiana, to do desk work. He hated it. As a member of the Training Administrative Division, Isaac spent all day every day processing the paperwork of soldiers going to Vietnam. To protest, he waged a one-man work slow-down. A few weeks later, several soldiers were killed by incoming artillery rounds within minutes of their arrival in 'Nam. They could not be immediately identified because Isaac had not done their paperwork.

As punishment, Isaac was forced to type all nineteen hundred pages of the processing manual in one week. When he failed to complete the typing on time, he was reduced in rank, removed from his desk, and given reassignment to truckdriving school. All day long, he was supposed to learn to drive a truck by wheeling one in and out of parking places in the base's gigantic parking lot. Isaac refused to do it. "Back home, I drove a logging truck from the age of fifteen. I don't need your goddamned school!" he told his commanding officer. As punishment, Isaac was given overnight guard duty. "Ain't nobody wants to break into this place!" he insisted. "A lot of guys want to break out!"

In the early morning hours, Isaac left his guard post, crossed a nearby highway, found a reasonably comfortable log in the woods, sat down and waited for dawn. When the PX opened, Isaac ambled in, bought a case of beer, a loaf of white bread, a can of Spam, mustard, pickled pig's feet, two cans of pork and beans, and an onion. He put all of it into a big carton, left the base, recrossed the highway, found his log, and settled in for a few days of peace and quiet.

In the meantime, Isaac's AWOL status had been discovered. MPs scoured nearby bars and whorehouses. Eventually, Isaac returned to his barracks. His commander was furious. He demanded to know where Isaac had been. Isaac told him.

The commander ordered a psychological profile. Isaac passed. "You're perfectly sane," the psychologist told Isaac. "The next time you go out there, take along a copy of this," and he handed Isaac a battered copy of Thoreau's *Walden*.

The commander again assigned Isaac an all-night guard duty.

"This time you'd damned well better be there in the morning!" the commander said, his voice a high-pitched squeal.

In the early morning hours, Isaac again retreated to his log. The MPs again scoured nearby bars and whorehouses. Again Isaac returned to his barracks a few days later. "It's nice out there in the woods—just like home," Isaac told his commander.

This time, at his commanding officer's behest, Isaac was imprisoned in a hospital for the criminally insane, but his stay was short. He was given an honorable medical discharge, and the psychologist who had originally profiled him gave Isaac copies of Emerson's poetry and the *Kalevala*. "As a Finn, you'll find meaning in this," he said to Isaac.

Isaac returned to Michigan and soon received the first of a life-long supply of disability checks. "You'll never have to work again," Peter told him. "What are you going to do with your time?"

"I'm going into the woods," said Isaac. "Thoreau did it, and he was sort of the ideal Finn. I want to live my life following his teachings. I want to be like Vainamoinen. I need to be away from people for a while. I need to find harmony in my life."

"Take a sauna," said Peter.

"I'll do that, too," said Isaac.

✿ ✿ ✿ ✿ ✿

Isaac obtained a mortgage through a bank in Houghton and bought himself an isolated piece of land on the west bank of the Yellow Dog River in the Huron Mountains and built himself a cabin and sauna. He blew up both bridges that allowed vehicles in summer to approach his property. The bridges were rebuilt, but nobody ever bothered him. He had made his point.

For the next twenty years, Isaac lived a seemingly uneventful life in the woods, though he himself saw every day of those long years as eventful. Isaac removed himself from most of the technology of the twentieth century and reclaimed a simpler world. He used only tools whose powers came from himself and the earth—an ax, a knife, a one-man bucksaw, hammers, wedges. His cabin was a half-day's walk from the nearest store. In summer, he carried in supplies in a packsack. In winter, he used a toboggan and snowshoes.

If something broke, he repaired it. If something was needed, he made it. His inventions were crude but usually worked.

In summer, Isaac gardened and fished. In fall, he hunted with a bow. In winter, he ran a trap line and snared small game—mostly rabbits.

A weasel lived under his sauna for two consecutive winters. He fed deer, birds, and squirrels, and once he saw a wolf cross the river below his cabin.

Mostly Isaac read. He ordered from remainder lists from a multiplicity of book dealers, and a steady supply of new books arrived at the little store a half-day away. The books covered every conceivable subject, but the majority furthered Isaac's need to be a better and better amateur naturalist and survivalist. He also read a surprisingly large number of books dealing with the meanings of things. Isaac saw himself as a seeker of truths. Tibetan Buddhism fascinated him. He saw its sacred texts as other versions of the *Kalevala*—full of earthy magic and personable magicians.

One January, Isaac tried to use the power of his own mind to generate body heat. Copying a Himalayan ascetic, he sat naked in his unheated cabin in a lotus position. He nearly died of hypothermia but felt at home with his long-dead mother just before he crawled into the preheated sauna.

Eventually, Isaac ran out of space and added a library to his cabin. The sauna was lined with bookshelves. So was the root cellar.

One winter, a starving fox broke into the library and ate Thoreau's seasonal journals.

Isaac began his own journals but soon gave it up. Who would read them?

When Peter was crushed by a tree he was felling, Isaac didn't learn about it for days. He missed the funeral, which was held at the Old Apostolic Church. Reverend Kinnunen, now an old, old man, pointed out in his service that Peter's blasphemy had finally caught up with him.

As the years passed, to the outside world, Isaac became a more and more fascinating eccentric—a recluse with an unknown history. Stories abounded about why he had gone into the woods. One said that he had been a famous scientist, on the run since the government stole his secrets. Another said that he was a lawyer disgusted by the world's corruption. A third said that he had been a millionaire, reduced suddenly to poverty. Still other stories said that he was running away from a woman or a crime. Local teenagers thought he might be a secret agent—CIA, Communist, or Nazi.

After Isaac died of natural causes in 1989, a folklore professor from downstate collected all the stories and put them in a book, along with photos of the cabin, the sauna, the library, and the root cellar. "What Isaac became will live on long after we are forgotten," the professor said in the introduction. Isaac had joined a pantheon of Finnish mythic figures. He was right up there with Vainamoinen, Heikki Lunta, St. Urho, and Paavo Nurmi. The Yoopers contemplated singing a song about him. The Oulu Hotshots memorialized him with a polka on a Saturday night in the Range Lounge. Soon he was studied in philosophy classes at Suomi College. He had his name on a bronze plaque in the Coppertown Lutheran Church. Little boys in Pelkie were named after him. An outdoor hockey rink in Toivola carried his name. His fame spread from Ironwood to Sault St. Marie.

✿   ✿   ✿   ✿   ✿

In the meantime, nobody knows where he was buried. Researchers say that his body might have been taken to a cemetery in Big Bay, or it might have been returned to Coppertown. Others say it's in Marquette or Houghton. The only thing that everyone knows for sure is that he's dead. His death certificate is in the archives at Suomi College, and archives do not lie.

Lauri Anderson was born and grew up in the Finnish town of Monson, Maine. He holds degrees from the University of Maine, Michigan State University, and the University of the Pacific. He has received grants from the National Endowment for the Humanities. A Peace Corps Volunteer during the Biafran conflict, he has also taught in Micronesia and Turkey. At present, he is Chairman of Language and Literature at Suomi College in Hancock, Michigan. He is the author of *Hunting Hemingway's Trout*, published by Atheneum, New York, 1990.

Other Finnish-American Titles
from North Star Press

Half Immersed   by Aili Jarvenpa
Poems giving insight ino the joys of tender childhood on a Minnesota farm with her Finnish immigrant parents.   ISBN: 0-87839-031-6   6.95

Finns in Minnesota Midwinter   by James J. Johnson
Cloquet native Jim Johnson writes with a particularly Finnish voice. In poetry he captures the lives and emotions of his Finnish grandparents and other immigrants.   ISBN: 0-87839-043-X   9.95

A Field Guide to Blueberries   by James J. Johnson
In poems, Jim Johnson provides striking images of how, when, and where to pick the "true blueberry." In the process, he weaves in his views of life, people, and the beauty of the North County.   ISBN: 0-87839-072-3   9.95

Helmi Mavis: A Finnish-American Girlhood   by Mavis Hiltunen Biesanz
This book describes the struggles faced by the northern Finnish communities to maintain their uniqueness as Finns while embracing the American way of life in the 1930s.   ISBN: 0-87839-052-9   12.95

Karelia: A Finnish-American Couple in Stalin's Russia 1934-1941
                          by Lawrence and Sylvia Hokkanen
In the 1930s Russia recruited American and Canadian Finns to come to Karelia, the "Worker's Paradise." The Stalin purges ended that dream for the Hokkanens, when they escaped and came home. After fifty years of silence, they tell their story of ideals, betrayal, and distrust.   ISBN: 0-87839-065-0   12.95

Isaac Polvi: Autobiography of a Finnish Immigrant   Joseph Damrell, ed.
With roots in post-feudal Finland, the Polvi family dreamt of a better life in the New World. Isaac was left behind for a year as the family settled in Calumet, Michigan. After a year alone, he rejoined his family and faced a life of mining in the United States.   ISBN: 0-87839-066-9   12.95

Gift: A Novel of the Upper Peninsula   Joseph Damrell
Isaac Polvi editor, Damrell enriches our lives and connects us to the Upper Peninsula in this wonderful backwoods tale exploring romance and mystery with Native American and environmental issues.   ISBN: 0-87839-071-5   9.95

In Two Cultures   Aili Jarvenpa, ed.
The struggles and successes of growing up in two cultures are described by thirty-five Finnish-Americans who grew up in two cultures and learned to appreciate the richness of their heritage.   ISBN: 0-87839-074-X   12.95

The Finn in Me:
The Chronicles of a Karelian Emigrant   by Sinikka Garcia
Forced from her home during the Winter War, Sinikka's family barely kept ahead of the bombs. Sinikka later immigrated to Mexico, where she married, then moved to the United States.   ISBN: 0-87839-070-7   9.95

Aleksis Kivi's Heath Cobblers and Kullervo   Douglas Robinson, trans.
The first English translation of Kivi's two most popular plays, both originally published in 1864. As a writer, Kivi has been likened to Twain or Dickens and is considered Finland's greatest writer.   ISBN: 0-87839-081-2   14.95